ADAM C. FRANCE

House on the Lake

of love and running

First published by ACF 2024

Copyright © 2024 by Adam C. France

First edition

ISBN: 979-8-99-073121-9

This book was professionally typeset on Reedsy.
Find out more at reedsy.com

Chapter One

Rounding the bend, the sun struggled to find its way through gray skies. Tamped gravel led the way down the path. Trees on the left created a canopy, blocking the view of the sewage culvert that flowed along the final six miles of the course. My feet moved forward slowly. I struggled to find air. Erratic breaths, wheezed in—and then out—and then in again, between parched lips. I blinked. I ran slowly. One foot, the next foot, each connected to tree trunks that once were legs. Heavy and awkward, I labored to keep my balance on the trunks that held me up and moved me forward. One foot forward. The next dragged and followed. I wobbled to one side, fought to regain balance—one stride, two strides, stumble, balance, step forward, stride, stumble, stride. My body was trained to continue moving, but had lost equilibrium and began weaving left, right, left... step forward, then back, left, then right, stumble forward.

Hands from behind grasped under my armpits and held me steady, yet continued to move me forward. A low gravely whisper, "Move forward. One foot. The next foot. Move forward." For some reason, my body listened. "One foot. The next foot. Move forward," the whisper came again.

I continued. Wheezing in. Wheezing out. Moving forward. Tree Trunks—balance—whisper repeated.

The whisper comforted, "Move forward. One foot. The next foot," as a cup of water was emptied over my head.

Water wetted my hair and dripped down my face.

Hands released my body.

I struggled to continue moving. Whisper repeated... "Move forward."

Hand gripped my wrist and urged me to continue. "Move forward. One foot. The next foot. Move forward."

Hand pulled me forward silently.

I began to move—to move more—to again move with a sense of purpose. Trunks began to lighten. Legs returned. Breathing slowed and regulated. I continued to follow the hand on my wrist. I gained strength with each step, enough to run as if my body knew where it was going.

Hand let go. Feet continued to move. Breathe in—Breathe out. Lungs filled and fueled my body. Feet moved forward.

The hand that held my wrist now ran beside me in tandem. It was Old Man #2. We ran together, quietly, but at a good pace and with life. Trees wished by on the left. Gravel crunched underfoot.

I managed my breathing and controlled my gait. My legs moved forward on their own, in stride, as they were trained to do. On cue, my arms began to churn with force, swishing, one and then the other, on opposite sides of my body.

I lifted my eyes and peered forward. Some ways off in the distance, I saw the end. The finish was near, within my grasp.

I picked up my pace. My strides lengthened. My breathing deepened and slowed. I begin to run without effort—my feet bounding, gliding, not touching the ground. I floated, I flew, I ran on clouds above the gravel pathway.

Striding forward, I felt nothing, save the wind through my body. All weight, all effort transformed into energy propelling me forward, faster and faster, to the end.

Trees ripped by on the left. Old Man #2 glided next to me, stride for stride. But I heard nothing.

Running continued. Feet moved forward, afloat, not touching the ground.

Without effort, I pulled myself in. My arms pumped. My legs floated, one in front of the other.

I was out of body, yet fully within and connected, totally cognizant of my weightlessness.

I ran free.

I came to the end.

I slowed down.

I walked.

I dropped to my knees.

Chapter Two

Our house was located a twenty-five minute boat ride from the edge of town. The boat launch was located just off the main road, next to a small donut shop and a park along the beach. The main burger place was across the street in an old cement building with walk-up ordering, a few dining tables inside, and a large sign in the parking lot that read, "Mama's Breakfast, Burgers, and Pies."

The road through town had one lane each way, a faded yellow line ran through the middle. It took about three minutes to drive from the beginning of town to the end, yet the road continued to wind along the bank of the lake, abruptly ending at a dirt road that led to the top of Lakeview Hill, a common gathering point for families on sunny weekends and teens on Friday and Saturday nights.

I would often go with my dad to the local grocery store to pick up food and then walk across the parking lot to the hardware store to load up on whatever was needed for the home. We made this trip a couple times a month during the summer and fall, maybe once a month, if lucky, during the winter.

We would carry a few bags from the store back to the boat launch, a walk that took us by the bank, gas station, and police department—I'm taking a bit of liberty calling the one-room building on the corner of Main Street and First a department. It was more like a phone booth. Open the door and a phone sat on a wooden table. Next to it, a chair and desk. Once or twice a week you might find the local fuzz sitting at the desk scribbling a few notes on his small black pad, otherwise, you would dial one of a couple numbers listed by the phone, hoping to track down Jim, our one officer of the law. During the spring and summer, the police force would grow 400 percent when Jim hired temporary help to keep an eye on the vacationers who frequented the town when the sun came out.

By the time we reached the edge of the boat launch, my arms would always be throbbing. The bags of supplies felt like someone had added bricks along the way. By the time I was 12, I could walk from the store to the boat launch without stopping, even though my arms felt like they were going to fall off. We would always take a break after we loaded the bags into the back of our beat-up 1960s, 17-foot cruiser. We would sit with our feet dangling off the side of the dock and crack open a couple root beers.

The boat belonged to my grandpa. My dad and his brothers used to take turns pulling each other behind it on their skis when they were teens. They would blow plumes of water behind them as they smiled and waved to boats passing by. Now the boat was just good enough to make a slow trek to town and back. The shine on the wood of the gunwale and bow had long since dimmed and the white stripes that ran along the side had faded to a cream.

I can still taste the suds of my A&W slide down my throat and tickle my nose. This was a treat. The only time we were allowed to indulge in the finer beverages that young kids crave was the trip to town for supplies. It was also the time that I got my dad to myself. At home, he was either busy in the orchards or his time was divided between me, Mom, and my two sisters.

We would sit there until we had drunk our root beers and exhausted the conversation. To me, it was never enough root beer or time with my dad. But I cherished it all the same. When I was small, just old enough to hop in the boat and travel with Dad for supplies, it would always seem like the adventure of a lifetime. My dad would turn the key and the sputter and splash of the outboard would signal the start of our next escapade. Now that I was 12, teetering on the edge of 13, it was different.

The experience had changed, and as I look back, the feeling of nostalgia fills my memories. At the time, I didn't understand what nostalgia was or that it even existed, but I can remember feeling that the trips were now somehow different. I couldn't tell exactly what that meant, but I remember missing how they used to be. Pictures flashed through my mind as I sipped my precious drink—Dad holding my hand as we walked on the dock, then scooping me up and placing me on his broad shoulders as we made our way to the grocery store.

Sitting there that day, I was aware it would be different from then on. I felt like I wanted to both hold on to the way it was, but also embrace the fact that I was becoming more independent. Yes, I still made the trip with Dad, but when we got to the grocery store on that day, he ripped the shopping list in half and told me to get the stuff on the list and meet him by the checkout counter. I felt proud. He trusted me to help out. But I also missed walking down each aisle, listening to my dad's jokes and stories.

With my root beer halfway gone, I found myself sipping slower than usual. I remember trying to make this trip last, just a bit longer. I had the sneaking suspicion that each trip would bring with it more changes and I would lose my little man connection with my dad. I could hear it in our conversation. He was asking me questions that felt out of place. Before it was Dad the Entertainer. He would reach down and tickle me, tell me a joke, and we would sit there laughing. Now, we were having conversations. He was asking what I thought. He was asking my opinions. It was both strange and made me feel good. While I wanted to remain my dad's little guy, this change was enticing. So, I sat there that day, dragging out my root beer for as long as I could, stuck between my six-year-old self and my soon-to-be teenage self.

"All right. Let's finish these things up and head back," my dad said in a jovial voice. I watched him take the last swig of pop from the can and squish it between his two hands. I stood up, lifted my can to my mouth, tilted my head back, and guzzled the last few mouthfuls of sudsy delight.

"Dad?"

"Yep." He turned and looked at me through his thick brown-rimmed glasses.

"This was fun."

"It sure was." He reached down and tousled my loose curls. A rush of little kid emotions ran through my body and I reached out and hugged him, with a bit more force than usual. I think I thought the harder I squeezed the longer this moment would last. "Let's go, bud."

We climbed into the boat. I untied the mooring line and placed it on the back seat. The motor sputtered its usual awakening call as spittles of water flew into the air and we slowly made our way out beyond the buoys and picked up speed. This is our only way to and from town, unless we wanted to ride our horses through the trails that met up with the main road at the top of Lakeview Hill, but that would take twice as long in the spring and summer, and even longer in bad weather.

I sat on the seat next to my dad, closed my eyes, and leaned back. The sun warmed my face and the wind kept me nice and cool. There was nothing I would rather be doing in life at that moment than riding the waves with him.

"Hey son, take the wheel." My dad's voice carried softly through the breeze. I stood up, looked at him, and smiled. I sidled in front of him, ready to guide us home, with my dad close behind, hand on mine. But this time, he backed off and took my place in the seat beside me. This was something new. Without warning, I was now the captain. I was charged with leading us, single-handedly, to our destination.

Normally we didn't talk a lot while the boat was moving through the water, leaving a small wake behind. We both enjoyed the sights and sounds of the wind and water and the noisy silence was like an old friend. But this time, I was eager to talk. I wanted to yell out, "Where is my old self?" But, as the boat continued to bounce through the small waves and the houses on the shore sped by, I felt myself moving, almost physically, toward that older me. I stayed silent while my grip on the helm tightened, as my grip on my new self took hold.

I was happy. I was gaining independence. I was becoming a young man, yet my dad was still by my side. I knew he was there and would always be there. He would give me space to grow, but he would never leave my life. This is how I knew I could move forward. This is how I knew I could allow my younger self to become a memory, a cherished set of memories.

The wind flew through my hair, as the sun warmed the back of my neck. I slowly turned my head from side to side and watched the familiar scenes pass by on shore. My best friend, Tim, lived a ten-minute boat ride from my place, across the lake on the south bank. I looked to my left and could see his family sitting on the lawn, too far away to discern any real detail. Up ahead just past his house was a faded gray wood building, the local school house. It contained three classrooms and a large central meeting area where we ate lunch. The school population was somewhere between thirty and forty students any given year. We were the Gray Wolves and every once in a while, we would have enough students to form an eight-man football team or a varsity basketball team. One year we had a good cross-country team. Well, actually we had Parker Thompson and four other guys who could at least finish a race. Parker won the small-school state title his junior and senior years, as well as, quarterbacked the football team, and was the leading scorer on the basketball team. Once he graduated, our boy's sports teams fell off the map. Most other kids spent their time fishing and hunting, both to put food on the table and because it was our way of life.

As the boat made its way closer to home, my hands automatically steered it to the left with relative ease as the north shore jutted out and created a cove that held within it a few docs and close to a dozen small homes. This is what we called the populated northwest end of the lake. Most homes on the lake were spread out by an acre or more. Here each house inhabited a quarter of that and the families shared much of the property, including orchards and farmland. It was somewhat of communal living. One family raised a certain set of crops and would share with the other families who had other essentials. It was an intimate living arrangement and made for a strong and safe life. If one family was in need, the others were there in support.

Lily Whitman lived in the first house on the cove. She was 13 and in the grade above me. She had a little brother and younger sister. Her parents grew corn and watermelon and had two milk cows. They made butter and cream. I enjoyed walking from the far end of the cove where my house sat on a sloping embankment, to her house, with two pails filled with apples and pears. Lily and I would run around their yard while her parents emptied my buckets and filled them with their homemade butter and cream. In the summer they would cut the end off a watermelon and we would dig in with two spoons, spitting the seeds across the yard.

On my way home, Lily would always escort me halfway and then head back to her place. I would usually turn and watch her walk for a bit before trekking the buckets to their final destination. She had a skip to her step and her light brown hair would dance in the breeze. We knew each other most of our lives. We moved to the cove when I was entering Kindergarten and Lily was the only kid close to my age that lived near me. Her dad finished building their house the summer before she was born. In fact, she was born in their living room just before the first snowfall of the year.

As the boat rounded the bend and the cove came into view, the houses seemed to welcome us home. I pulled the throttle toward me, half expecting my dad to change places with me as we approached our dock. But he didn't. The motor slowed to a deep hum and I maneuvered the rig sideways and then forward. My dad jumped onto the dock and secured the boat in place. I cut the engine and listened to it sputter, spit, and then finally lay silent.

We grabbed our provisions and headed to the end of the dock and up the stairs toward our weather-beaten blue and white bungalow. The original house we moved into was small, but my dad built an addition on the back that added quite a bit of space. The old house had two bedrooms, a kitchen, and a living room.

The addition added two more bedrooms, a second bathroom, and a large room with a fireplace.

We trudged to the top of the stairs and around the back of the house. We opened the wooden gate and headed to the storage shed, winding our way through the chickens and goats that stood in our path. We had an old cold storage crate in the back of the shed where we kept most of our dry goods. Whitie, our old gray mama goat, walked over and nudged me softly with her head before I could make it into the shed. She followed me a few steps and waited outside, hoping for a handful of feed when I emerged. As I came out, she perked up, but then noticed I didn't intend to feed her, so she nudged me again, but this time with a bit more intent. "Okay, Mama, I know. I'll be back out in a few minutes to feed you." It was always her. She led the pack. She was the leader who always reminded us it was feeding time.

While Lily's family made butter and cream with cow's milk, we made goat cheese and pasteurized a bit of milk. We always had a few goats and chickens strolling around our yard. We loved it when it was goat cheese time 'cause we knew Mom would soon be making her ultimate macaroni and cheese—a delicacy if there ever was one.

Dad and I unloaded the rest of the food and supplies in the kitchen and then I headed back out to feed Whitie and the rest of the animals. We were the only ones home at the time. Mom and my sisters were at a birthday party for one of my sister's friends. Since we took the boat into town, they walked the half-mile to the end of the cove to the Johnson's house. The Johnsons were an older couple who adopted their granddaughter after something went wrong with their daughter. I never knew the whole story, just that, one day the granddaughter showed up without her mom and never left.

Whitie met me at the back door and strolled up to me with a look of determination. I knew she wasn't going to let me get away this time. She nudged me with her head and then rubbed the side of her body against my leg. We walked over to the shed. She waited patiently as I entered. When I reappeared, I was carrying a pail of feed and was suddenly surrounded by a small herd of goats, our usual lot, plus a small kid we named Runt. He was born a couple weeks earlier.

I spread out a few handfuls of seed on the ground. My new admirers lowered their heads and focused their energy on the sustenance strewn about.

As the goats inhaled their food and their bleating became muffled, I repeated the same ritual with our chickens, this time making sure to keep the food in a designated chicken coop. When I was given charge of the feeding my dad gave me strict instructions, "Keep the chicken feed in their coop. Goats will get sick if they eat chicken feed. It's okay if the chickens eat a bit of goat feed, but goats can not eat chicken feed." I followed my dad's instructions. I wasn't sure why, but by his stern look, I knew it was important.

The chickens pecked away at the ground as I locked the gate. I turned to see the sun fading behind the west hills, the diminishing light reflecting a pinkish glow off the billowy clouds. I walked over to the opposite side of the yard, just outside the entrance to our orchards. Last weekend, my dad and I put up a hammock between a couple old trees. It felt like the right time to give it a trial run. I sat in the middle of the green fabric, steadied myself, and then slowly swung my feet up and lay down. The hammock closed in on me, enveloping most of my body, save for my face and the tip of my toes.

A light wind rocked me back and forth the slightest bit. It

reminded me of lying in our boat on calm water. It was quiet, for the most part. I could hear our goats rustling around in the distance, but other than that, I felt the calmness of early evening.

I closed my eyes and took a deep breath. Seldom did the serenity of our lakeside home seem so close. The hustle and bustle of the day always started with early chores and ended the same way. So, I took advantage of the chance respite and drifted off.

I woke a bit later to the banging of pots and pans through the kitchen window. I slowly opened my eyes and noticed a darkened, pink sky overhead. Light broke through the patchy cloud cover and dimly lit the path to the house.

I swung my feet over the edge of the hammock, sat up, and felt for the ground with my outstretched toes. I stood up, raised my hands in the air, and stretched as I connected back to reality.

I made my way through the backdoor, turned the corner, and walked into the kitchen. Steam rose from the stove as my mom stood at the counter, cutting carrots.

"Hey, Mom. How was the party?"

"It was nice. The girls enjoyed themselves. Would you grab a clove of garlic from the pantry and cut it up for me?"

"Sure." I turned and opened the cupboard door behind me and rattled around until I found the small tan object. "Was Lily's family there?" I asked as I grabbed a knife from a drawer and began my not-so-graceful chopping of the pungent vegetable.

"Yup, they were..." she answered, with a sly grin on her face. "Lily has sure grown up over the past few months. She must be an inch or two taller than you now."

Hmmm. I thought to myself. *She probably is.* "Oh, I haven't noticed. I mean, she seems the same to me." My mom looked at me out of the corner of her eye, and let out a hushed little giggle.

"Sweetie, make sure to dice the garlic nice and small. You know your sisters don't like biting into big chunks."

I bent over the garlic and focused. I worked on moving the knife faster up and down, careful not to get too close to my fingertips. I finished chopping and scraped the pieces into a small bowl. "I think this will do," I said proudly.

"Looks good, son." Mom gracefully took the bowl and poured the garlic into the pot on the stove. She added the carrots and a couple handfuls of potato chunks. "You run along now. I'll have dinner done in a little while."

"Thanks," I said quickly, and then headed out of the kitchen, down the hall, and into my bedroom.

I plopped down on my bed and lay there. Staring up at the ceiling, an image slowly emerged in my head as I began thinking about what my mom said about Lily and why it was so important.

I looked closer at the image. I focused on it as if I were trying to decipher an ancient code recently uncovered. I saw in my mind, Lily, walking back to her house, hair blowing in the wind. I found myself deep in thought, trying to decode the image. A feeling of wonderment came over me. I connected my mom's words with my desire to watch Lily as she walked away. This was a relatively new habit of mine. And, for some reason, I thought about her more now. In fact, she was on my mind more often than not.

Chapter Three

I woke up, two years after the day I sat with my dad on the dock, sipping our root beers. It was the last summer before I took the big step, back into the small schoolhouse, yet this time as a high schooler. Ninth grade was coming soon and I had made a pact with myself. I was finally going to tell Lily how I felt about her. I spent the last two years standing back, admiring her, but so had a few other boys in our small town and I didn't want anyone else getting in my way. At the end of the school year, Lily went to visit her cousins and wouldn't be back for a couple of weeks, so I had some time to build up my courage and I was glad. I didn't have a clue what I was going to say.

In the meantime, it was a nice sunny day. I woke about five AM, dressed, and went outside to do my chores. I hated getting up early, but if I didn't, the animals would go hungry. It took me about an hour to feed the animals and clean their pens. The nice thing about summer was, I could always jump back in bed and catch up on some much-needed teenage snooze time. But, this morning there was no time to go back to bed. I was planning on meeting up with Tim. We were going to work on the old car his grandpa gave him and we're hoping to have it running by the time we were old enough to drive around here, which was a bit earlier than usual. There were a few unpopulated dirt roads we could explore between our homes, except none of them actually connected our houses, so we could never drive from one to the other. But, at least, there was one road that went from his house to town, so there was a bit of a connection to civilization.

I was planning on spending the day with him, working on the car and asking him for some advice about Lily. I hadn't told anyone about Lily yet and Tim was the only person I trusted with this vital information.

I usually rode my horse to Tim's place, which took about thirty minutes. It was only ten minutes by boat, but even though my dad let me drive the boat, he didn't let me drive it alone yet. Living half an hour from my best friend is one price I had to pay for living in what mom called "heaven on earth." Standing on our front porch as the light stretched its first few rays over the hilltop and across the lake was nothing short of miraculous. The natural beauty of our lake was surpassed by nothing, except, in my mind, by the beauty that lived just a few houses down the cove. And, other than helping Tim with the old car, my goal in life was to muster up the courage to tell Lily how I felt.

I finished spreading the seed and cleaning the pens. Back in the house mom had just started breakfast. By the time I changed my clothes, washed my hands and face, and walked into the kitchen, there was a stack of pancakes and fresh boiled eggs on the counter. While I was cleaning the goat pen, I saw mom pulling a few eggs from the mamma hens. She is really particular about her chickens. She makes sure the coop is in pristine condition and that the eggs are cleaned properly. Boiling the eggs helps to make sure that any bad germs are gone. She says that it's easy to transfer disease from chickens, so it is important that I do my part each morning and clean the coop. I peeled and bit into one of her boiled eggs and was reminded why it was worth getting up at the crack of dawn every morning to tend to my chores.

With a full stomach and a hug from the cook, I headed out to the barn to check on Jeffy and get him ready for the ride. About a year ago my dad got me a quarter horse from a family on the other side of the lake. Their youngest son had recently moved across the country, so they were shedding a bit of weight, getting rid of a few cattle and two horses.

My dad said it was time I had something of my own to take responsibility for. I was excited, initially, until I figured out how much work it was. I was in charge of everything, from running him around the paddock every day to feeding, grooming, and cleaning his stable.

I named him Jefferson, or Jeffy for short, because my younger sisters were studying the presidents at the time and I had just helped them memorize the first ten presidents for a test. Jefferson was our third horse, so I figured I would name him after the third president.

Jeffy was almond-brown with a beige patch between his eyes. He was fourteen hands and was probably just under a thousand pounds. When we got him, he looked a bit chunky, so my dad told me I had to exercise him at least twenty minutes each day during the week and a ride around the hills behind the house on weekends. There was a trail that led in a circle that took us maybe forty minutes, so we usually did that once and then explored a few of the other trails close to home. Once Jeffy was in better shape, I was gone upwards of two to three hours. The first few months, though, it was a chore just coaxing him around the first loop.

I remember often meeting Lily by her place and riding to the edge of town. When the trail narrowed I would let her lead her horse on ahead, while I followed behind and watched her ponytails—and a few other things—bounce from side to side. And one day, as I watched her ride, I made up my mind, I would find a way to tell her how I felt.

I found Jeffy in his normal spot, rear-end greeting me as I walked in, his head poking out the open window at the opposite side of his stall, taking in the sights and sounds in the yard.

"Morning, boy. "

His head slowly turned. He peered at me from the corner of his right eye. I'm sure he was checking to see if it was worth expending the energy to turn all the way around, looking closely to see if I was holding a carrot or an apple. He obviously decided that meandering slowly is all that was required this time and then shyly bowed as I stuck out my hand and patted him on the head.

I stood on the gate railing and spent a few minutes rubbing his neck. I dismounted, grabbed a brush off the wall, and joined him in his stall. I opened up his feed trough where my dad had already loaded some hay. I usually fed him in the morning when I fed the goats and chickens, but on the days I rode, I found he had more energy toward the end of the ride if I didn't feed him too early.

He walked over with an awakened gait, dropped his head, and gnawed away at his meal. I took the time to go over his body with the brush, massaging his back and sides with the stiff bristles. This always seemed to rouse him and get his blood flowing.

I pulled his saddle pad down from the wall, shook it out, and combed through it with my hands. I inherited the pad from my grandpa when my dad got me the horse. It used to be a dark brown, but Grandpa was an avid rider before he hurt his hip and wore it down to its current weathered gray. He used to go on trail hunts almost every weekend. Depending on the time of year, he was hunting for his next meal or scouting trails for future hunting trips. I still remember holding tight to my grandpa's waist as we rode double through the bush scouting a turkey run. I was about eight years old. Not long after, he fell off his horse and hurt his hip, ironically hunting turkeys just a few weeks later.

By the time I had the saddle pad ready, Jeffy had eaten his fill of hay and walked over to me. There was life in his eyes. With a good brushing and a full belly, he was ready to hit the trails. I arranged the saddle pad on his back and lugged the saddle from the rack. When I first learned how to saddle my horse I had to stand on a small stool, but since then, I'd learned to use my hips for leverage and was able to pop it up and place it gently on his back. It took some time to learn, but my dad spent quite a bit of time helping me figure it out.

I situated the saddle so it sat firm and then reached down and laced the strap. I double-checked everything once I was done because early on I had a couple messy rides as the saddle loosely swished from side to side.

I adjusted the strap one last time, guided the bridle over his head, and opened the pen gate. I took hold of the reins, led Jeffy to the edge of the yard and tied the rains to a tree. I grabbed the saddle bag from the back porch, looking inside to see what goodies mom had packed for me. On the days of my long rides, mom usually packed me a couple sandwiches and something to drink, and sometimes even a change of clothes—and of course, my pocket knife, a trail rider's best friend. Even though I was only going to be riding for a half an hour, she still included her normal PB and Js and a thermos of water.

I walked back to Jeffy and secured the saddlebag, untied him from the tree, and hopped on. I situated myself on the saddle and off we went. We always started slowly, as it usually took me a little time to feel confident and it was good for Jeffy to warm up his joints. A few minutes in, I took her up to a trot and then eventually a slow gallop. My amateur skills and the hanging branches overhead usually kept me tame.

Right before we reached Tim's place, the trail opened up into a small field and I felt a little courageous, so I let Jeffy run free. My heart pounded as he galloped the last two hundred yards. I listened to the wind rush by my ears and the rhythmic four-beat-thud of his hooves strike the compacted dirt repeatedly before we finally slowed down and came to a walk at the fence line that edged the property. I spotted Tim and his dad through a few trees in his front yard. They were bent over his car and I heard the echo of tools being put to work.

"Looks like you're working hard," I yelled from a distance. Tim's dad popped his head around and shined a big smile my way.

"Just getting her started for yuh," he said as he held out a big wrench in my direction. "She looks a little shabby at this point, but nothing you boys can't handle."

I dismounted and tied Jeffy to a stump in the middle of the yard. "I'm sure we can handle it Mr. Samuelson." I stuck out my hand and smiled as he deposited the wrench in my underdeveloped palm.

"Well, boys, I'ma get me some coffee. I'll bring you some cider in a bit." He pulled a handkerchief from his back pocket, wiped his brow, and headed inside.

"Thanks, Dad," Tim said as he walked out from behind the far side of the car and turned to me. "How's the trails today? Thought we might take a ride before dinner."

"Pretty good most of the way," I replied. "They were a bit soggy by the creek though, but not bad everywhere else."

"How you like riding your horse? Tim asked. "I haven't seen him since you first got him."

"We're getting along well. I was able to run him in the field."

"Yeah, I heard you coming. He has a nice gallop."

"Her old owners used to do some trail racing with him, but that hasn't been for a couple years."

Our conversation meandered along as we dug deep into the engine of the tired '54 Chevy Bel-Air. Tim told me it had been sitting in his grandpa's barn for a number of years. The red sheen had faded to a flat pinkish hue. The whitewalls were a dusky gray and the chrome hubcaps and trim were covered by a few layers of dirt. While I didn't know much about cars, Tim learned a lot from his dad and grandpa. He explained that it was an inline six or "straight six," as his dad called it.

We worked on the engine for a couple hours, then took a lunch break. I shared my sandwiches with him and his dad brought us some drinks and a carrot for Jeffy. The sun camped overhead as mid-day approached. We untied Jeffy and walked him around for a bit before we got back to work. I was more of the grunt, following directions, but it was fun and I learned quite a bit. Tim would remove a piece and tell me how to clean it or oil it or take it apart. I would keep my hands busy while Tim's head was under the hood. It was the beginning of what would be a long but fun couple of years.

We finally came to a stopping point, cleaned the tools and put them away. Even though I enjoyed working on the car with Tim, I kept thinking about Lily. I was nervous to talk to her about how I felt and now I was nervous to tell Tim. That was new to me. Tim and I shared everything. It was strange. I was actually feeling a bit queasy.

We walked over to the side of his house, turned on the hose, and took turns scrubbing the grime off our hands.

I finished up, tossed the hose on the ground, and turned off the spigot.

"Hey, Tim?"

"What's up?"

"Well..." I cleared my throat and took a deep breath. "I wanna ask you something."

"Something wrong?"

"Nah, but, I want to ask your help."

"Of course."

"You don't even know what it is."

"Don't matter. That's how we are."

"I know, but this is different." I looked up at the sky.

"Come on, man. Just let it out."

"Well..." I paused. "You see, it's about Lily."

"You mean, you gonna ask her out?"

"What?—No—I mean—yeah—How'd you know?" I laughed awkwardly.

"Man, it's obvious."

"What you mean, it's obvious?"

"I see how you look at her. You sure as heck don't look that way at me."

"Do you think she knows?"

"Not sure, but she might."

"Shit." I looked at the ground and shook my head.

"Oooh. Must be a big deal if you're willing to swear." He chuckled and slugged me in the shoulder. "It don't matter if she knows," he reassured me. "It won't change nothin'. You guys been friends for most your life. Most people think you guys are a couple anyway."

"What do you mean?"

"I mean, well, maybe not literally, but you do spend an awful lot of time together. Outside of me, she's the only person you really talk to."

"Yeah, I guess you're right."

"It's okay man. I'll help you figure it out. When she gettin' home?"

"Probably about two weeks."

"Perfect. We have some time to think about it. Let's hit the cove tomorrow and go over some ideas."

"Great, you still owe me a race to the rock," I flashed him a rye smile.

"You looking for an ass whoopin'?" He flexed his muscles and danced in a circle. We laughed.

When he stopped showboating, I popped my arm around his shoulder and looked at him. "Thanks man. I've been bustin' my brain trying to figure out what to say to her."

"Fuck yeah, man. Of course. We always stickin' together."

Tim headed behind the house to the barn to get his horse. I untied Jeffy and walked him around the yard as I waited.

That evening, we rode through the trail that wound around the trees near his house. It was much like that the next two weeks. We worked a few hours each day on his car, then we rode horses as the afternoon turned to evening, with the occasional dip in the lake at the cove by my house or a long brainstorm session on the sand, warmed by the day's sun, discussing Lily.

As the days slowly marched on, my nerves grew more intense and I was sure I would never muster the courage to talk to Lily about my feelings. But, as futile as it seemed, I continued to dream of her and rattle my brain.

Chapter Four

The days seemed jam-packed. I had no schedule, yet I was always running from one thing to the next. And I was glad to be busy, as any idle time was filled with thoughts of the girl who lived on the other end of the cove. I would lay in bed at night and she was on my mind. I would feed the animals in the morning and her face was all I could think about. This made time crawl from one minute to the next, so it was nice to have things to keep me occupied and delay those thoughts, even if only for a short time.

On one of my trips to Lily's house to deliver pails of fruit, her mom asked me to come in for some fresh-baked bread. Lily's brother and sister, Billy and Sam, were sitting at the table in the kitchen, each with a tall glass of milk and a thick slice of bread. They had full mouths, smiles on their faces, and yet still had the ability to talk and laugh without spewing all over the table.

I sat in an empty chair. Lily's mom brought me a thick slice of bread and a glass of milk. I thanked her sheepishly, as I was mustering up the courage to ask her when Lily was coming home. I had spent quite a bit of time with Lily's family over the years, but this time I felt awkward and uncertain. And while I sat there letting the fresh bread dissolve in my mouth, I was trying to find a way to weave Lily's name into our conversation.

"Wow, this is really good, Mrs. Whitman," I said as I wiped my mouth and took a swig of milk.

"Thanks. You're welcome to have another slice. I'm so used to baking for a family of five and with Lily gone, we always have extra."

There it is, I thought, *my chance to slip in the question*. "Yeah, sure. I'd love another piece." I paused for a few seconds, and then cleared my throat. "So, Ahhh... When you expecting Lily home?"

"Well, she was supposed to come home on Tuesday, but she's been helping her uncle with some work on the farm and asked to stay until it is done. So, my guess is another week or two."

I stopped chewing momentarily as my heart felt like it suddenly rose up and collided with my Adam's Apple. I felt sick to my stomach. I was in a daze and didn't know what to say next. I sat silently for a few minutes, hoping my stomach would settle down as I finished the remainder of my bread and milk.

When I was done, I took a deep breath and let it out slowly. Billy and Sam were still nibbling at their bread and laughing away, at what, I wasn't sure. All I was thinking about was how I would survive the extra two weeks of agony. I pushed my chair back from the table and stood up. I wanted to tell Mrs. Whitman I missed Lily, that I wanted her to come home. I wanted her to know that I had something important to tell her and it couldn't wait. It was amazing how, after all these years, this moment seemed so important. I suddenly felt anxious. My breath quickened and I was sure Mrs. Whitman could hear my heart beating faster and faster as I stood there trying to control my emotions.

"You okay?" Mrs. Whitman asked. "You look a bit tired."

"Oh, yeah. I spent a lot of time in the sun with Tim yesterday and I got up early to get my chores done today."

"You take it easy on your way home."

"I'll probably go to bed early tonight. I've been helping Tim work on his car the last couple weeks and we're planning on starting early tomorrow."

"That sounds fun. I haven't seen Tim for a while. You should bring him around sometime. We'd love to see him." She picked up my empty plate and cup and walked them over to the sink.

"Yeah, I might do that. Maybe the next time we go swimming in the cove." I walked over and leaned on the counter. "We're actually almost at a stopping point 'cause we're waiting on a new alternator and some headers his dad ordered. We'll be going down south sometime in the next couple weeks to pick 'em up. But until they get here we'll probably have more free time."

"How's it going little man?" Mr. Whitman's voice filled the kitchen as he entered, rolling up his sleeves. He walked over next to Mrs. Whitman and washed his hands. He always referred to me as "little man," ever since the first time our families met. "I've got your pails filled with the milk and cream. Tell your parents the cream is good for the next two weeks. It was churned yesterday."

"Thanks Mr. Whitman." *And remember, I'm not a little man anymore*, I thought to myself. Even though the term of endearment felt kinda good, and I really liked Mr. Whitman, I wanted him to be ready for this young man to be hand-n-hand with his daughter soon.

As I walked outside and grabbed the pails from the back porch, Mrs. Whitman stuck her head out the door. "Remember to bring Tim by while you're waiting for the parts."

"Will do Mrs. Whitman." I turned to head home, but peered over my shoulder and yelled, "Thanks for the bread."

"Anytime. " She smiled.

About halfway back, I acknowledged Mrs. Whitman. "Yup, I'm a bit tired," I said to the blowing breeze. And then took a deep breath, wondering if I would ever get the chance to unload the emotions weighing me down.

* * *

Dinner that night was good. Mom made chicken pot pie and peach cobbler. We mainly grow apples and pears in our orchards, but we grow just enough peaches to have good desserts now and then. But, while the food was more than satisfying, I couldn't do much but spoon the food into my mouth and think about how I was going to make it through the next two weeks. I didn't know how I was going to survive. At least dad's stories helped pass the time around the table. Tonight he gave us his harrowing rendition of the emergency call to the vet to deliver the breached calf a couple years ago. This story could be categorized as a fish tail. Each time he told it the fish was bigger and heavier than the last. Once, it was his arm that was buried deeper inside the cow and another time the vet, who was only in town twice a week, had to brave rain, ice, and snow, just making it to the barn with minutes to spare. We never corrected him, but it was always funny to watch mom's wry smile and the twinkle in her eyes as she listened to her husband spinning his yarns, a little longer each time.

Chapter Five

The next week felt like a month. I needed to find a way to move the clock forward, or at least get my mind, and my racing hormones, under control. With at least a week left until Lily got back, I decided to go to bed early so I could help time speed up. What I really wanted to do was sleep through the next seven days. But, I woke early, like usual, quickly attending to my chores and eating breakfast, and then I was out on the trails on my way to Tim's.

When I got to his house, it was quiet. I was earlier than usual, so I tied Jeffy to the stump in the front yard and walked around the back of the house to his bedroom. "Yo, Tim," I whispered at his open window. "Hey, Timmy," I said a little louder. I heard some rustling inside and then a soft groan. I could see a shadow through the half-closed blinds. The darkened figure sat up.

"Ahhh..." a sigh wafted my direction. "What you doing here so early?"

"Thought we could ride into town before we get started on the car."

"I think the back door is unlocked." He rubbed his eyes and yawned. "I'll meet you in the kitchen."

I sat down at the kitchen table and watched dust particles dance in the dawning light peaking through the shades. The smell of bacon filled the house. I assumed his mom had already cooked breakfast for his dad, who worked for the forest service ten miles outside of town. There house was modest, but they were proud of their home. They both came from meager upbringings and worked hard for everything they got. I looked up to them and, in fact, saw them as a second set of parents. They welcomed me into their home all the time and took care of me and my two sisters when our parents had to leave town to tend to our grandma who passed away from cancer. I almost felt as comfortable here as I did in my own house.

"So, what're we riding to town for?" Tim burst into the room with newly discovered enthusiasm.

"I don't know. I'm just restless."

"You mean you can't get Lily off your mind and you want me to entertain you."

"Of course. That's what you're good at."

"I just wanna let you know, I have my own women to think about and you woke me up from my date." He let out a playful laugh. "So, if we're going to do this, you owe me a coke and a donut." Tim was amazing at getting our minds off our troubles and if all I had to do was buy him a drink and his favorite chocolate donut, I was game.

The donut shop was our regular stop when we hit town. We always bought day-olds. We loved how the crusty icing crumbled in our mouths, and we didn't mind that they were half off either.

Tim poured two cups of coffee from what was left of his dad's breakfast and we sat at the counter, sipping quietly, my mind frantically rolling in circles.

"Okay," I said, breaking the silence, "Let's get going."

"Shit, man. What's the rush?"

"You know, I can't stop thinking about her," I replied in frustration.

"I do hear some donuts calling my name," Tim said as he yawned and stretched his hands to the ceiling.

We gulped down the last of our coffee and headed outside to gather our horses. Until we got the car running and we turned 16 we couldn't take the Bel-Air into town. So, the next best thing was a canter on the back of our horses.

The dirt road from Tim's to town was just a couple miles. Sometimes we would take a detour halfway to visit Joey's place, but he was out of town for the summer. Joey is another one of our gang. We would get together with Joey and a couple other guys to go hunting in the fall or hit the cove by my place on the first warm day of Spring. Joey was a head taller than everyone else in the school. He shot up early and was close to six feet tall by eighth grade. He started growing hair under his armpits before anyone else and he even had a few whiskers on his chin. Tim and I still seemed to be quite a ways away from puberty, at least it looked that way from appearances. The three of us joked a lot about how long it would be before we would ever touch a razor, while Joey was already running his buck knife across his face daily.

The sun had been up for a few hours by the time we set off for the donut shop and the heat was radiating from the compact dirt when we reached the outskirts of town. I could tell it was going to be another scorcher as a trickle of sweat ran down my back. We were on the opposite side from where my dad and I docked our boat on shopping days and had to make our way through the park and a few old buildings before we got to our destination—a small weathered outhouse, a large metal utility shed, and the grange, where birthdays, weddings, and Fourth of July celebrations were held.

Our horses made the transition from dirt to blacktop and we clomped our way along the side of the road and through the middle of town until we saw the market. The donut shop was just on the backside of the parking lot, behind Mama's Burgers. The smell of sugar and frosting made our nose hairs stand at attention and led us to our morning meal.

Our mouths began to water and, as if trained to do so, our stomachs began to gurgle simultaneously. We were Pavlov's dogs and the sweet aroma was the bell calling to our olfactory senses.

Recently, Dad shared the story of Pavlov and his famous experiment when I asked him why Whitie started whining before I even made it to the barn to feed her. He said that she was conditioned to whine and then went into a five-minute diatribe about this famous experiment that happened sometime in the late nineteenth century. I didn't much care at the time, but it made more sense as we approached our culinary destination that morning. My dad had a way of educating us without our even knowing it. A conversation about something that seemed trivial would turn into a short history or philosophy lesson, and at some random moment in the future, his words would creep up on us and come to life.

We tied our horses to the gate and went inside. There were a few people milling at the counter and the tables at the side of the dining area. The owner's radio was playing the local station and the tinny sound of rock music mingled with soft conversation. We looked around to see if we recognized anyone. During the school year we would invariably see a friend or family we knew, but in the spring and summer months we often didn't know a soul around as the streets and businesses became home to out-of-towners who came for the beaches along the glacial waters of the lake.

We sat down with a couple of day-olds and some Cokes. It was quiet, yet the murmur of voices could be heard over the high tap of the drum beat in the background. The man behind us was talking about taking his boat along the south shore. The kids sitting at the far end of the counter were giggling about something, while a family sat at the far side of the shop in silence eating their donuts diligently.

"Let's ride down by the beach," Tim said matter-of-factly. "I'm sure we'll find something to do down there." I threw him a shy smile. He nodded and winked. He knew I knew exactly what he was getting at.

There were a number of beaches along the shore in town, but there was only one that was worth our time in the heat of the summer. Jackson's Inlet, named after one of the first settlers in the area, was the beach closest to most of the rental cabins where vacationing families would flock. There would usually be a few girls around our age laying out at the edge of the water or on the dock a few yards offshore. If I didn't know any better, I was sure he was trying to get my mind off Lily, and considering my options, I was game. *Never hurt anyone just to look*, I thought.

With sticky fingers and a bit of energy, we left the donut shop, hopped on our horses, and headed out. We rode past the beach, and as predicted, the sand was packed with people. We stopped at the edge of an embankment that rose high above the beach where a few kids were gathered taking turns jumping into the icy waters twenty feet below or swinging from the rope tied to the huge Hemlock that leaned precariously over the edge.

We tethered our horses and joined the group at the swing. A few familiar faces mingled with vacationers. Yelps and splashes made their way through the air as kids flew to their destiny below. We weren't really there for the festivities, even though we would take our turns on the rope. We had come for the vantage point. From our perch, we could see from one end of the beach to the other and could scope out the entire scene.

As we waited in line for our turn to fly, we huddled together and talked our way through the scene below. We saw some friends from school swimming along shore, a number of families with small kids, and what looked like a birthday party at the barbecue pit. Not much in the way of girls our own age. While that didn't bother me much, Tim had a perplexed look on his face. I would like to say he was thinking about me, but knowing him he was looking for a conquest for himself, but finding none, felt the pang of disappointment.

"Ahhh..." Tim said under his breath as he scowled at the people below.

"Don't worry man, it's almost your turn. I'll give you a good shove so you can do a backflip."

"Yeah, like last time. I was feeling the sting on my stomach for a week."

We stood, waiting, as the line continued to shorten in front of us. We stripped to our shorts, leaving our shoes and clothes in a pile. Suddenly, out of the shadows of the Hemlock, a soft, high-pitched giggle floated through the air like gentle notes of music. We turned around. Two figures stood in the darkness of the tree.

We stared into the dark shadow as two girls, in their bathing suits, walked into the light and got in line behind us. As cool as we thought we were, we were too dumbfounded to say a word. We each gave it our best to stay composed, just long enough to watch two guys join them and our attempt at some sort of composure was visibly lost. We turned to each other, wide-eyed, shaking our heads.

We made our way to the front of the line, knowing that this was our chance to show the ladies behind us what they were missing. Although, I'm not sure Tim's belly flop and my high-pitched squeal did the trick. But, anyway, the refreshing water helped jar us back to reality and Tim's original reason for leading us to this spot. We swam to shore, began our trek along the edge of the water, and scanned the crowds of people.

We gave a couple head nods to people we knew while we kept our eyes peeled. The waterfront at the inlet was maybe a couple hundred feet long, so over the next fifteen minutes we made our way back and forth a couple of times. By the time we made it back to our splash point under the rope swing, we could feel sweat rolling down our backs, so we took a swim out to the dock to cool off.

We swam out and grabbed hold of the ladder on the edge of the dock. There was no climbing up as people were piled on top of each other sunbathing or waiting for their turn to be pulled behind their boat. This was the most popular ski spot, partially because there was a wide expanse of water connected to the inlet, but also because it was a perfect place to show off for the crowds on the beach.

Legend has it that a young boy drowned under the dock after he dove in and got trapped underneath and it creeped me out, bobbing up and down in the water there. People say his screams could be heard all the way to the north end of the lake. I felt like there was something floating just below my feet. Some people even say they never found his body. *Was the whole thing just a made-up ghost story or was his body still lurking just beneath the surface?* I had a difficult time keeping my cool and I didn't want

Tim to sense my anxiety because he wouldn't let me live it down.

Tim was always the brave one. I remember the first time I spent the night at his place. We were in second grade. We spent the entire day tramping around the woods by his house, making a hide out between two fallen trees. We found an old blanket and a tarp in a pile of garbage hidden beneath a bunch of debris about a mile from his home. We dragged them back to our hidden location and erected what we felt was a fort for the ages. We used some ivy vines to tie the tarp over the top of the trees and spread the blanket on the ground. We found an old wooden box for a table and some moss we used to pad the ground beneath the blanket. It was amazing. Our own place. Our hideout.

Before dinner that night, we finished the last few details by camouflaging our fort with pine tree branches. If you stepped away and looked directly at it, even knowing it was there, it was hard to see. We were proud. We knew we had made something special. And as we trudged our way back to Tim's house, we couldn't stop talking about all the cool things we would do in our camp; late-night campouts, staging battles with the enemy, building a second room, maybe a place to hide our valuables, whatever those were to a second grader.

We barely made it through his front door before we heard his mom bellow, "Hold on you two. March back outside. I want those dirty clothes off in the laundry room. You have ten minutes to get washed up and ready for supper." We looked at each other and laughed, then headed around back and stripped to our underwear in the laundry room.

After dinner, we spent the next hour in Tim's room reliving the exploits of the day. We talked about the first time we were going to spend the night on our own out in the dark, dense woods behind his house, and all the cool things we were going to do.

We knew if we asked his mom if we could sleep in our hideout, she would say we were too young, so our conversation was a plan for some time in the future.

Silence ensued, but I knew we were both thinking about the same thing—crawling through the woods, hunting for food, protecting our hideout from any intruders that may pass. We lay in the quiet for a few minutes... and then... all of a sudden, Tim sat up.

"Let's just do it," he said in a low, determined voice.

"What do you mean," I replied, eyebrows furrowed.

"Let's go out there and spend the night."

"You mean without asking?"

"Yeah. We'll go when my parents fall asleep."

At eight years old it never crossed my mind to do something without asking our parents. And here he was, as determined as ever, acting like he was ready to take on the world.

It had never occurred to me that the day we were going to sleep in the woods would actually arrive or, more importantly, would be that day. I never knew that sleeping in the dark dense woods by ourselves would be a reality. It felt like we were talking about dreams, about the exploits of one of our favorite characters in our comic books. I was so detached from the reality of our dreams that I didn't even think about the fact that what we discussed would take some amount of courage.

It was at that point I noticed the difference between Tim and me. He had a built-in courage that I lacked. I had to grab on to his and hope it would keep us both safe, as, that night, by his bidding, we snuck out in the dark and slept amongst the nocturnal creatures. And this was just the beginning of the adventures that Tim initiated over the years.

Tim let go of the ladder and disappeared into the water. He

stayed submerged for what seemed like an eternity and then popped up behind me. I turned around quickly, just as he took a deep breath and spit a plume of water into the air. "EEEEYA," he shouted at no one in particular. He stretched his arms above his head, looked around, and gave me one of his big smiles. "All right, man. Let's get back to the beach and catch some rays."

We turned toward shore and began extending our arms through the water as our feet splashed behind us, gliding forward until our toes reached the rocky ground. We stood upright and trudged through the water and onto dry sand.

We found an open spot and plopped down. I closed my eyes as the back of my head lay on the soft ground and drifted off into a light sleep. The sound of the wind and waves mixed with the cheerful laughter of young kids and their parents comforted me as my body warmed. The sun was right overhead. I could feel the heat drying my body as I lay, half in a dream and half attuned to the world around me. A speedboat whipped by in the distance. The buzz of the outboard sang loudly and then dissipated until it was gone. Kids cannonballed from the dock. Light footsteps caressed the sand as they passed by above my head. And then, I was suddenly dead to the world, somewhere deep inside my own mind.

Sometime later, my ears began to open and reality slowly seeped in, until, with my eyes still shut, I was wide awake. I heard a conversation taking place nearby—just behind me and to my left. I lay still and listened. It took me a minute to figure out who they were. I didn't know them. Or at least, I didn't recognize their voices, but I could tell they were female.

Their soft voices gently drifted into my space. My ears perked up. I felt the hairs on my arms stand on end. The words themselves didn't matter. The cadence of their voices, the sweet giggles that bounced in and around their words made my heart rate quicken. I could feel a rhythmic thud deep in my chest.

I lay motionless for a long time. Their conversation quickened, stopped, began again with a new energy. Silence. The ruffling of sand. Footsteps above, beside, now in front of me. I slowly sat up and propped myself on my elbows. I opened my eyes and let them adjust to the light. I squinted and panned the sand in front of me, looking to put a vision to the voices. And there they were. Standing just a few feet away. The girls from the rope swing. They stood, side by side, looking at each other, laughing and smiling.

My eyes were first drawn to the girl on the left, her red hair past freckled shoulders and halfway down her back. She wore cut-off blue jeans and a blue bathing top. Her skin had a slight red glow from a day in the sun.

Her friend wore her dark, curly hair short, just above her ears along the sides and above her shoulders in the back. She had a darker complexion, as if her skin was used to being in the sun. And while I first noticed the bright hair and complexion of the red-haired girl, something about the girl on the right was breathtaking.

The girl on the right—I paused in mid-thought as I tried to figure out what it was—the girl on the right wore a slight smile on her face, but the smile came from her eyes. There was a sparkle, a twinkling that emitted from her gaze—a happiness that enveloped the air around her.

I watched as the two stood close to one another trading what seemed to be intimate secrets only they could understand. Then, they turned and bounced toward the water—my eyes fixed on the girl on the right. Her red flowery swimsuit cupped her buttocks just enough to tantalize my heart, but revealed only a first impression, while my mind made up the rest.

I took a deep breath and looked over at Tim, still lying in the sand. I stood up, stretched my arms to the sky, yawned, and then wiped the sand from my legs and shorts. I panned the shoreline. Kids splashed at the water's edge. A dog walked by, lifted its leg, and urinated on the wet sand.

I turned back to Tim. He was still asleep. I thought about waking him and having him join me in the water, but on my first move toward the two girls who stood knee-deep, splashing water on each other, I mustered up the courage to go it alone.

I entered the water, just a few feet away from the girls. I walked past them until the water came up to my waist. I turned to see what they were doing, but they didn't show any sign of noticing me. I squatted down and let the water cool my body, my eyes still fixed on the girls, and continued down until my head was submerged. I held my breath as long as I could, hoping that when I surfaced the girls would miraculously turn their attention toward me.

I came up, took a deep breath, and knelt down on my knees so the water was hovering under my chin. I tried to act nonchalant, slowly moving my head from left to right and back again, as if I was checking out the people on the beach. Yet, as my head panned back, they were gone. "Hmmm," I grumbled to myself with disappointment and then stood up and looked over at Tim. He was now sitting up looking off into the distance.

I walked over and sat next to him. "Did you see those two girls?" I asked.

"You mean those two," he chuckled, nodding in the direction of two heads bobbing up and down in the water making their way toward the dock. "I saw you trying to get their attention. Smooth, man," he said with a sly smirk. "I didn't think you had the nerve."

"Shit. I got some moves."

"Yeah, they seemed to notice," he bellowed, bending over, head between his legs, shaking with laughter. I grabbed a handful of sand and dumped it on his head, stood up, and dashed for the water.

"Oh, you asking for it, boy." Tim ran toward me and tackled me in the water. He gave me a couple playful punches to the side as we splashed around awkwardly.

We came up, gasping for air between laughs, and simultaneously turned toward the bobbing heads and found them at the dock, each with an arm extended, hands holding onto the ladder.

"So, this is better than sitting at home waiting for Lily to get back, eh?"

I paused, shrugged my shoulders, and let out a quiet, "Mmm, maybe."

"Well, let's change that attitude." He dove under the water and came up, swimming swiftly toward the dock.

"Ah, shit," I said to myself. I shook my head and dove in after him.

Halfway there Tim stopped. He looked my way and smiled, "You coming or do I have to embarrass you myself?"

"Fuck you," I retorted, ducking my face into the water and speeding toward him.

As we reached the dock, the girls had found one of the few open spots to stretch out on the wet planks. We pulled ourselves up and found a sliver of space, just large enough to prop ourselves up on the edge. The dock was full. At least a dozen people sat, lay, or waited on the edge for their turn to be pulled behind their boat.

We waited patiently, hoping that someone would depart the

floating mass, giving us a chance to get closer to the two beauties lying peacefully on the far end.

We talked quietly, hoping not to be overheard. "You gonna make the first move?" Tim whispered.

"I'm not sure what to say, but there's something about the girl with the short hair."

"Really? I thought you would go for the redhead."

"Yeah. She's hot. But, the other girl... there's something about her."

"That's fine with me. You just gotta make the first move. If you leave it up to me, you may not have a chance with either of 'em." I reached over and shoved his shoulder. "I mean, with my charm, I'm liable to run off with both of them," he added.

A boat pulled up alongside the dock. Waves splashed up the side and sent the dock up and down. Two people jumped in the boat and a third strapped on a ski and grabbed the handle of the tow rope. The boat roared off and our opening beckoned. Tim popped to his feet and began his strut to the other side. I jumped up and followed awkwardly.

The girls sat with their feet dangling over the edge of the dock, waves lapping at their ankles, looking off to the distant shore. We sat down, squeezed into the open space, and were now close enough to touch them. Tim eyed me, nodded his head, and waited.

My mind raced. *What do I say? What if they tell me to get lost or laugh at me?* I took a deep breath. I heard the air going in my nose. Pause. Exhale. I heard the air escape my pursed lips. "Excuse me," is all I could muster. "Excuse me," I repeated. They turned. "Didn't we see you at the rope swing a little while ago?" I said sheepishly.

"Probably," the redhead answered.

"I thought so." I felt a bit of courage emerge.

"Are you guys on vacation?" I continued.

"Sort of... I mean, I am," the redhead answered.

"What about you?" I turned my attention to the short-haired girl.

"Well, my parents just bought some land up the lake near the cove."

"Oh, I noticed some activity at that vacant lot not too long ago. Was that you guys?"

"My parents bought the plot next to the house on the cliff." She smiled.

"You mean the one with the Gray barn in the back. That's my place."

She turned toward me a bit more. "Wow, you mean we're neighbors?"

"If you're going to live there we are." I paused for a moment. "You guys building a house?"

"Right now my mom and I are renting one of the cabins down here on the beach. My dad will be bringing our trailer to the property in a couple weeks and then we are going to set up camp. He says we'll start building our home next spring."

"Cool. Welcome to our lake."

"Thanks."

"We'd love to show you around sometime if you'd like."

"We?"

"Tim and me—Oh, yeah, this is my best friend, Tim."

"Hey," Tim interjects.

They turned and smiled his way.

We found out that they were from a town 200 miles south. Tanya, the redhead, was staying for the summer while Jade got settled into her new surroundings. Jade was entering the ninth grade and was going to attend our school in the fall. When I heard the news, my heart began to pound and I found myself hoping my face wasn't as red as it felt. *Maybe it will blend in with my tan*, I thought.

We sat and talked a while longer, trading tidbits about our lives and then the girls mentioned that they had to be back to the cabin to meet Jade's mom. I felt a quick pang in my stomach. I didn't want them to leave. I wanted to come up with something to say that would persuade them to stay a bit longer, but, before I could, they stood up and jumped in the water.

"Jade, " I called, as her head popped to the surface.

She turned and looked at me, "Yeah."

"Whatcha doing after dinner?"

"Not much."

"Uh, how 'bout we come by your cabin and take you guys on a tour? We can show you a shortcut to the cove."

"Sounds fun. We're in cabin #3. How about six o'clock?"

"See yuh then," I said, trying to contain my excitement.

Tim nudged me with his elbow and shot me a smile. "What about Lily," he scoffed. I returned his smile and shoved him into the water. I joined him with a cannonball splash and we made our way back to shore and climbed our way back up to the big Hemlock and the rope swing where we found our clothes still sitting in piles next to our horses.

We dressed, mounted, and rode our way to the watering hole on the other side of town. We let our horses bend their heads and lap at the fresh water and then walked them over to the adjacent field and waited while they joined a few other horses, grazing among the grass.

We sat in the sun watching our horses and mused about the day's events which ended with a chance meeting with two beautiful girls and my soon-to-be neighbor. I could feel the grin on my face and the blood pumping through my veins as our conversation meandered along.

As we sat there, we both admitted to hearing the other's stomach, reminding us that the last meal we had was day-old donuts many hours ago. So, we dug into our pockets, counted what money we had left, and headed to Mama's Burgers in the middle of town. We had just enough to each scarf down a double Mama's Burger and a root beer, and we shared a bag of Mama's Curly Fries covered in ketchup. We sat at a picnic table outside the drive-through window for a while, watching the vacationers going in and out of the building. We said hi to a couple of friends from school, Todd and Lester, who were going to be seniors. They told us that our school was going to try to field a full cross-country team this year. There was a new kid that just moved in that was supposed to be pretty good and they thought we could have a shot at a small team state trophy. They knew we were both decent athletes, so they worked us over pretty good, telling us all the benefits—getting out of school early, traveling with girls... and, um, and, well, I'm trying to remember any more benefits, because all I could think of was running every day until my legs fell off.

We slapped high fives with Todd and Lester as they jumped on their bikes and peddled off. "Think about it. We start practices the last week of August," Lester yelled, just before they turned the corner and disappeared behind the building.

Tim looked at me with a quizzical look on his face. "Cross-country, huh? Never really thought about it—maybe."

I shook my head, "You ready for them hills behind the school? I watched them training a few years ago. The year they won the state title. That didn't look like any fun to me."

"I'm not thinking about the hills. I'm thinking about girls and that trophy."

"I heard the first week of practice the coach works you until you throw up. They call it 'the garbage can run.'"

"Yeah, I know about the garbage cans. I heard Parker Thompson fell into one of the garbage cans head first he was heaving so hard."

"And you would actually do that?" I questioned, eyebrows raised.

"I don't know. Maybe. For girls, I would do quite a bit."

We turned and peered at the clock on the wall inside Mama's Burgers. "Just about five thirty," I said. "Let's make a pit stop and then head to the cabins."

We walked around to the back of the building. The door to the bathroom was ajar. As we entered, we had to squint to let our eyes adjust to the diminished light. I relieved myself in the urinal while Tim's flow splashed loudly in the stall. I zipped up, washed my hands, and looked into the mirror. A reddish-brown face looked back at me. I was surprised how much darker I had gotten, as I hadn't looked at myself for almost twenty-four hours. My normal Scandinavian skin was taken over by my Cherokee blood. I turned the faucet on again and stuck my head under the running water. I pulled my head out and let the water drip down my face and then ripped some paper towels from the dispenser and lightly dried my hair. I peered back into the mirror and arranged my hair in a more presentable fashion. Tim finished up and met me outside.

We walked back out front and gathered our horses, leading them for a while before we jumped back on. When we reached the campsite, we dismounted and tied our horses at the gate. We made our way through some tent and trailer sites and passed the outhouses and a small communal pool. Splashes and screams could be heard echoing through the trees as families and their kids made use of the chlorinated retreat.

The cabins were just off in the distance past the pool and behind a small group of new-growth evergreens, planted by the senior class as a present to the camp owner who donated the use of the camp cabana for the prom a few years ago. The cabins were separated by a few trees and a slatted fence. A round, rusty iron fire pit, a wooden picnic table, a car stall, and a post to tie a horse were in front of each. A pump spigot sat in a central location, offering potable water for campers to share.

We passed the first two cabins and approached the third. As we got closer we heard laughter and soft music and saw smoke lofting into the air. We peeked around the trees and saw our new friends sitting at the table, a small campfire, recently smothered, was gasping its last breath.

"Hey guys," Tanya said as she stood up from the table. Jade, whose back was to us, turned, and I felt a tingling emerge in my stomach.

"Great, you're here," Jade giggled. "My mom just took off to meet with a friend. Let me throw some more water on the fire before we take off." She grabbed an empty jug and walked up to me and took my hand. "Help me fill this." She tugged on my arm, "Come on," she said playfully. I followed, a bit clumsily as she led the way, still clutching my hand in hers.

"So, you said your dad is coming in two weeks?"

"He has to finish a job before he can make the move. My mom needed to be here to sign the final paperwork for the land."

"What's your dad do?"

"A bunch of stuff. He builds houses and for a while he was running a farm outside of our town. So, that's what he's going to do here. He says the land here is perfect for grazing."

"Oh, yeah. There's a nice pasture at the back of the property and it's already partially fenced. There used to be an older family who had a couple trailers on the property, but a few years ago their family came and got 'em and cleared everything out. "

She stopped just before the spigot, turned, and looked me in the eyes. "To be honest... I'm scared."

"Oh?" My voice cracked.

"I've never lived in a small town like this before and my parents have been going through some rough times. It's just such a big change and I'm not really sure how my parents will handle it, being so far away from everything. Really, I'm not sure how I'm going to handle it."

I looked down at her hand still holding tightly to mine, my tan skin a few shades lighter than hers. "Hmmm, well, I'm a small-town boy, for the most part. I've spent a couple summers in the city with my cousins, but other than that, this is where I grew up."

"It just feels so strange," she said softly.

"There's actually a lot to do around here," I said reassuringly. "You ever been hunting?"

"Nope."

"Do you like to fish?"

"When my dad took me a couple times."

"There's also a great horse riding trail that leads through the woods and around the lake. You can ride from the end of town, past the cove, and to the other side of the lake."

"I've never ridden a horse before."

"That's how we got here today. Our horses are tied up at the front of the camp."

"How you planning on showing us around?" She asked, a bit

surprised.

"I guess you'll just hop on behind me and hold on for the ride. I take my sisters on trail rides all the time."

"You have sisters?"

"Two younger sisters, nine and eleven."

"That must be nice."

"How 'bout you?"

"I have an older brother, but he's been off fighting fires for the last three years, so I don't see him much."

"That's cool... the fighting fires part, I mean." I looked down at the ground and then back to her.

She smiled at me, squeezed my hand, and let go to take hold of the pump handle. "Here, let me do that, I said, scurrying up to the spigot." She held the jug under the faucet as I pumped the handle. Water gushed sloppily out of the nozzle as we stood in silence, listening to the gurgle of the jug as it filled. I stopped pumping and took hold of the jug as we made our way back to the cabin.

"Horses, huh?" she questioned.

"Yup, horses," I replied.

"Took you long enough," Tanya called out as we appeared from behind the trees.

"Wonder why?" Tim quipped.

Jade and I looked at each other, shrugged, and let out a little, knowing laugh. We felt a bit closer. Maybe from the sharing of a few intimate details, but maybe also from knowing that we're now pretty much neighbors. Soon, her family would occupy their new plot next door to my family. She will occupy a space between me and Lily, the girl I spent much of my life growing up with, much of the last couple of years fawning over in secrecy. Even so, for some reason, I felt a sudden connection to Jade, one that, curiously, I felt she shared.

I poured the water into the fire pit. Small billows of steam floated from the ashes.

"Let's head out," Tim said as he rose from the table.

"Where we going?" Tanya asked.

"First off," Jade exclaimed, "it's not where we are going. It's how."

"Huh?" Tanya looked at her quizzically.

I turned to Tim, "Did you tell her how we make our way around town?"

"Oh, you mean the horses?"

"Horses?" Tanya questioned, shaking her head.

Jade turned to Tanya, placed her hand on her shoulder, and laughed. "Yup, you heard him right."

"Well, I guess I'll trust you," Tanya said to Tim.

"You ain't got nothing to worry about," he replied, as he turned toward us, arms spread wide.

We wound our way through camp and found our horses, still tied up safe at the entrance, and spent a few minutes giving the girls some pointers about riding double on horseback. They were nervous at first, but as we talked, their nerves gave way to a bit of excitement.

We mounted and pulled the girls up behind us. Even though I gave my sisters rides all the time, this was different. Jade nudged up against me, leaning her cheek up against my back, clasping her arms tightly around my waist. I felt the tension in her body, but more importantly, I felt her soft breasts between my shoulder blades. We started off with a walk, taking our time as we made our way out of the camp. I turned my head to the right and asked Jade how she was doing.

"Fine," she replied and I felt her relax her arms around my

body.

I urged my horse to a trot to catch up to the other two who were just ahead of us. I felt Jade pull herself closer as she jostled up and down behind me. I pulled up alongside Tim, slowed the horse back to a walk and told him to lead us to the top of Lakeview Hill. He nodded and I could see him turn and say something to Tanya, who looked like she was clinging on for dear life, eyes squinted shut.

We passed our meeting point at the beach from earlier that day. I pointed toward the lake and described the scenery to Jade—the homes on the south shore across the water, the reservation on the hill above the houses, the boats docked at the Yacht Club which were barely visible far off in the distance.

We continued to the end of town, following the fading yellow-lined street until we passed the old houses that butted up against the dirt road that led through trails speckled with a few houses and then on to Lakeview Hill.

We sat on our horses for a few minutes looking over the lake. A couple families sat on blankets by old BBQ pits, kids sitting on laps and cuddling with mom and dad after a long day. From atop the hill you could see the expanse of the lake as it drifted, diminished, and vanished both East and West. Trees lined the shore and ran up the hill on both sides of the water. Houses were scattered throughout the trees, many of which were only occupied two seasons, Spring and Summer. You could see the top of the school building nudged between trees on the Southwest shore, just before the lake vanished behind a bending of waterfront and trees. We explained that the school was built thirty years ago on the hillside central to where most people lived and hidden behind the school was a small field for sports and gym classes.

"If you ride this trail for another forty minutes or so, you'll reach the cove," I told Jade. "My dad and I make trips to town on our boat a couple times a month to do our shopping."

She looked at me a bit perplexed, "Where's the road?"

"There's no road. You follow the trail. It's by horse or foot."

"It sure is beautiful. At least it's got that going for it," she said in consolation.

The lake traffic was slowing down. We could see a few boats running across the water, leaving white ripples behind. A family of four gathered their blankets as the mosquitoes began their nightly ritual. They mounted their horses and slowly trotted by. Small, dark creatures darted to and fro in the waning light of the sky. Fruit bats signaled the time to head back. There was about an hour of light left before the sun found its resting point behind the hills.

"Welp," I called out quietly. "We should take you guys home."

"Hmmm..." A soft sigh of disappointment came from the rider still clinging to my waist.

"We can always pick this up tomorrow. If you're free I mean." I anxiously waited her reply.

"Yeah. We were just planning on much of the same. A day at the beach and maybe a walk around town," Jade replied. "What do you think, Tanya?"

"As long as Tim can put up with me," she giggled.

"If I don't have bruises around my ribs from you squeezing me so hard, I'll be surprised, but I'm willing to put up with you for another day," he laughed, turned, and gave her a quick kiss.

We turned and made our way down the hill, leaving one family roasting marshmallows over a fire. The obtuse thud of our horses' gait turned to a sharp click-clack as hooves met with paved road. We meandered home, horses walking at a leisurely pace, and made our way through the middle of town, and then turned into the campgrounds. We stopped at the gate, dismounted, and secured the horses.

Tim slung his arm around Tanya's shoulders and I grabbed Jade's hand. We walked around the gate and headed to their cabin. My heart pounded as I thought about leaving her for the night. *Do I say goodbye? Do I thank her for a fun time? Do I kiss her?* My hands began to sweat as we got closer to cabin #3.

Tim and Tanya stopped near the water spigot. Jade and I continued walking. As we neared their cabin, Jade tugged at my arm and pulled me behind the trees that separated cabin #2 from cabin #3. She turned toward me and threw her arms around my neck. "That was fun, " she said, looking directly into my eyes.

"Yeah, it...." She leaned in and interrupted me with her soft lips. Surprised as I was, I fully embraced the moment, as I wrapped my arms around her waist and pulled her close. We slowly leaned back, just far enough to look each other in the eyes. I finished my interrupted thought, "Yeah, it was fun," and we stood there, quietly. The moment felt natural, like we were supposed to be together.

"I don't feel as nervous about moving to this tiny town now." She paused for a moment and looked up at the sky and then back at me. "Thanks."

I wasn't quite sure what to say, still focused on her lips. I fumbled—"Yeah. For sure." We stood, looking at each other for a moment. "How 'bout we meet at the donut shop tomorrow? I asked. "You know where that is?"

"Yeah. We walked by it this morning before we went to the beach."

"Okay, how 'bout nine?"

She leaned in and pecked me on the lips. "Sure. We'll see you tomorrow."

We walked around the tree to find the other two sitting at the picnic table. I saw a figure walk by the lighted window of cabin #3. "Looks like your mom's home," I said.

"I'm sure she's wondering where we are," Jade replied. She skipped over to Tanya and grabbed her hand. Tim and I watched as they waved and headed inside.

In twenty-five minutes we were at Tim's house and I was on the phone with my dad, letting him know I was going to stay another night at Tim's place. He told me that I owed him one for taking care of my chores for two days. I promised him I would do double duty when I got home the next night, then lay back on Tim's bed and fell asleep.

Chapter Six

The next morning I woke early. Tim was still snoring away, so I got up, threw on my clothes, and headed out to the kitchen. Tim's mom was making coffee and I could see his dad outside in the front yard through the kitchen window.

"Morning, early riser," Tim's mom was always cheerful, no matter what time of day. "You up for some pancakes?"

I yawned and rubbed my eyes, "Yeah, sure, thanks." I stretched my hands over my head, trying to wake my body.

"Take a seat at the table. I'll bring you some OJ while you wait."

I sat down, still in a bit of a morning fog. I would have loved to dive under the covers for an hour longer, but my mind, even in its grogginess, was racing with thoughts of the coming day.

"Here you go." She set a large glass of orange juice in front of me.

"Thanks." I sat there for a few moments, staring at the glass and blinking my eyes.

"You still look half asleep. Whatcha doing up so early?

"Uh, I don't know. Just couldn't sleep."

"You feelin' okay?"

"Yeah," I said through a yawn. "I sometimes just like waking up with the morning," I said, trying to conceal my eagerness to start my day with Jade. "I'm used to getting up and doing my chores before the day gets too warm."

"Me too," she replied. "And don't worry, your pancakes will be ready in a couple minutes. You like your bacon crispy, right?"

"Yes, ma'am."

"I thought I remembered you picking the crispy ends off the plate last time you were here."

I ate a heaping stack of pancakes, some eggs, and that crispy bacon, and then thanked Tim's mom. I headed back to the bedroom and found Tim, still sawing logs, so I jumped in a shower and cleaned all my crevices, even between my toes, so I would look presentable. I walked back to the bedroom as I ran a toothbrush through my mouth. I peeked in and saw that Tim was gone and I could hear his voice in the kitchen.

I joined Tim at the table as he scarfed down his breakfast. I turned and peered at the clock over the stove, seven-fifteen. *Hmmm.* I thought to myself. *Maybe I should have stayed in bed longer.*

That morning felt like molasses. By the time we set off on our horses, it felt like a whole day had passed. We told Tim's parents we were meeting some friends at the rope swing and would be gone until suppertime. His mom made us some sandwiches and his dad handed us some money. "Just in case," he told us.

We made our way down the trail and into town. The streets were just waking up. We could see people going in and out of the grocery store and a couple cars parked at Mama's restaurant. While Mama's was known for burgers, you could get a good breakfast there too. My family made a trip into town every once in a while for an early meal. My mom and dad love Mama's biscuits and gravy and my sisters and I usually got the waffles or pancakes. For some reason, the trips to Mama's with the family always felt like special occasions. We all cleaned ourselves up, jumped in the boat, smiling and laughing the entire way. I'm not sure what made it such a big deal, but it was. And as Tim and I passed the burger joint that morning, I cracked a smile.

We arrived at the donut shop, tied up our horses, and peered in the window. The girls weren't there yet, but by the clock on the wall inside, it was not quite nine, so we sat at one of the tables outside. The sun on my forehead was already palpable. That wasn't anything new this time of year, but, even so, the heat made the wait that much harder.

We sat for a few minutes and then looked around. The girls were nowhere in sight. I began to wonder if they would show. My heart sank. I turned to Tim. "You think they'll show up."

"I hope so," Tim said as he looked off into the distance. He took a deep breath. "Why wouldn't they." He shot me a half smile.

Suddenly, a horn honked and a small Toyota pulled up beside us. My heart raced as the car door opened and the girls got out. "Bye, Mom," Jade called as they walked toward us. A hand reached out of the driver's window and waved. The car turned out of the parking lot, just as the girls walked over and plopped down at the table.

Jade was wearing a blue baseball cap, a pair of cut-off jeans, and a white t-shirt. Her dark skin sparkled in the sun and her jet-black curls were poking out from under her hat. Tanya got up and walked over to Tim. "What do you guys have planned for us today?"

"Got to start by getting a couple day-olds. That's why we're starting here," Tim answered.

We stood up. I took Jade's hand and led her inside. As the door opened the usual Top 40 music from the radio filled the air.

There were a few people sitting at the bar and a couple families spread throughout. I waved to Jody behind the counter. We've known her ever since her family bought the place a few years back. They moved up here from down south somewhere. Jody was the owner's wife. She always saved us the good donuts from the day before.

As we entered, I noticed people turning our way and looking at us. I didn't think much of it, except for the fact that Jody, who was normally friendly, didn't wave back.

We sat at a middle table, between a family with two kids and an older couple. I recognized the family. I think their kids were in the elementary class at school, but the older couple must have been on vacation because I hadn't seen them before.

"So, what do you want?" I asked the girls. "We usually get a couple chocolate donuts and a Coke, depending on what they have left over."

They didn't answer right off. Jade lowered her head a bit and slowly scanned the room. "Are we okay to eat in here?" she asked.

"Whatdaya mean? We eat in here all the time," I said.

"Just get us whatever you're having," Tanya replied. "We'll just sit here quietly." She turned and gave a reassuring look to Jade.

I walked to the counter and looked in the glass display. Jody walked up to me, head cocked back, chin raised. She was wiping her hands on a small towel tucked into her apron belt. "Who're your friends?" she inquired.

"A couple girls we met at the beach yesterday."

"Huh," she huffed. "They staying long?"

"What do you mean?"

"How long they in town for?"

"Jade's family just bought the land next to ours on the cove. Said they're building a house soon."

"Jade, the redhead?" she questioned.

"No, that's Tanya. Jade's the other one."

"I see," she said under her breath. "Whatcha gonna have?"

"We'll take four long chocolate ones and four Cokes."

"Why don't you guys wait outside and I'll bring them to yuh."

"Uh... no thanks. We'll eat inside." I furrowed my brow and looked at her. She grumbled something inaudible and walked away. "Here's the money," I said, putting a five-dollar bill on the counter.

"Just leave it there. I'll bring yuh your change."

As I headed back to my seat I felt eyes following me. I looked around. People had stopped eating and had turned all attention to me. I wasn't sure what was up.

I sat down and looked at Tim. "What's going on?" I asked.

"I'm not sure," he replied.

"We should probably eat outside," Tanya whispered.

"Huh... What's wrong?" Tim asked.

"Let's just eat outside," Jade added.

"Okay. If you want to. You guys head out. I'll grab the food." I stood up and walked to the counter, "Hey Jody. We'll eat outside."

"Good choice," she replied, handing me a tray and twenty cents change.

As I headed out the door, all eyes were still glued on my movements.

I walked over and set the tray on the table, my three companions sitting in silence.

"I got you each a six-inch chocolate." Still, they sat in silence. "And a Coke," I added. Still nothing.

I looked at Tim as I handed them each a donut. I nodded my head and mouthed, "What's going on?"

Tim took a deep breath and paused. "The fuckers were looking at Jade."

"Jade?"

"Well, really, they were looking at you."

"Me? What did I do?"

"You were holding her hand."

"Okay?"

"And they didn't like it," Tanya added.

"They didn't like what?"

"Come on. They didn't like you holding my hand," Jade said softly.

"What?" I said in disbelief.

"You remember when the Joneses moved in on the east end of the lake?" Tim asked rhetorically, breathing deeply, face visibly red. "Well, remember how these people reacted to them? To their different look?" He paused and took a deep breath. "These people don't like you holding Jade's hand. You get what I'm saying?"

"What the fuck?" I said in disbelief. My normal calm demeanor was quickly transformed.

"Remember when I said I wasn't sure about moving here," Jade said, tears welling up in her eyes.

"Those fuckers," I broiled. "I'll kick their asses."

"No, leave it alone. Let's just get out of here," Jade added solemnly.

We sat there silently for a moment, my blood boiling. I looked at Tim, who was steaming on his side of the table holding Tanya's hand, and then I looked back at Jade, tears slowly rolling down her cheeks. I stood up, slammed my hand on the table, and stormed over to the door, pulling it open with all my might. I stood there, and looked around at all the white faces in the room, trying to catch everyone's attention. "I'VE EATEN MY LAST DONUT AT THIS PIECE OF SHIT PLACE." I paused briefly. "KEEP YOUR GOD DAMN CHOCOLATE DONUTS TO YOURSELF, YOU BASTERDS..." I stood there for a few seconds, hands on my hips as an exclamation, underlining and highlighting my angry words. Everyone just sat there. Jody stood still behind the counter, a soft drum beat from the radio was the only noise to be heard.

I took a deep breath, turned around, and made my way back to my friends. Tim had a big smile on his face. He stood with one hand on Tanya's shoulder. Tanya sat there motionless, holding Jade's hand. I looked at Jade, not really knowing what I was doing or how she would react. She just sat there, a frown on her face, droplets of tears standing still on her cheeks. I knelt down in front of her and put my hands on her knees. I looked straight at her face. She slowly turned toward me, a faint smile curling up at the edges of her mouth.

* * *

We spent the rest of the morning and afternoon riding along the trails that took us to the south side of the lake, passed Tim's place, and to the school. We stopped at Tim's house to get something to drink. Luckily his parents were in the back pasture, so we didn't have to introduce them to Jade and Tanya.

At the school, we showed them around the outside of the building that housed the classrooms and then took them to the field in back. We climbed to the top of the wooden grandstands that graced the home side of the football field and rested for a while. A small rudimentary dirt track circled the field, faint white lines rounded the track and could just be made out if you looked hard enough. On our way back we took them to the woods behind Tim's place and showed them where we built our first hideout in second grade. Decrepit as it was now, it was still there, and we assured them that it used to be a palace. They laughed, but sympathized with us a bit and agreed that it must have been grand years ago.

Jade held tightly behind me as we rode the uneven paths around the lake. We walked in the woods and around the school holding hands, talking and laughing, Tim and Tanya always nearby. We didn't talk about the donut shop once.

On the way back into town we stopped just before the dirt met the pavement, dismounted, and walked the horses to the edge of the lake. We sat on the grassy shore as the horses lapped up the water. The sound of boats was like a hive of bees off in the distance, adding to the soft ambiance that cradled the afternoon in splendor. We sat, two couples, breathing in the sun-drenched air. We said few words, yet we communicated much. The warmth of the afternoon sun, the comfort of our bodies lightly leaning on one another, created the perfect ending to our day.

I looked down toward my outstretched legs, Jade's feet intertwined with mine. I looked off into the distance, the north shore just visible from our low vantage point. The beach where we met just a day before was almost directly across from where we sat relaxing.

Tim got up, went over to his horse, and reached into the knapsack attached to its side. He pulled out the sandwiches his mom made for us that morning and the four of us shared a simple, delightful moment, watching the glitter of the water and the waves lapping against the shore.

I leaned back and rested my head on the ground. Jade lay back, her head on my outstretched arm. I pulled her close. We stared at the blue expanse and watched the few billowy clouds float by. I raised my hand and pointed at an eagle gliding high above.

Tim and Tanya stood up. Hand-n-hand they walked over to a rock formation that jutted out of the water. They removed their shoes, waded into the water, and sat on the boulder, dangling their feet and ankles deep into the ripples.

I closed my eyes.

"Thank you." A soft whisper in my ear. I turned and smiled. She was looking directly at me and smiled back.

A few minutes later we gathered our horses and made our way to the paved road and through town. We passed the grocery store, Mamma's Burgers, and eventually, the scene of our morning encounter.

We said nothing and then continued to the girls' camp.

We tied our horses and walked to cabin #3. I told Jade that I had to catch up on my chores at home and didn't know the next time I could make it to town. She ran into the cabin and quickly came out with a pencil and a piece of paper. She asked for my phone number. I wrote it down, smiled, and gave her a kiss.

Ninety minutes later I had dropped Tim off at his place and made it home. I lay on my bed, the smell of Mom's meatloaf filling the air. My mind wandered through the last twenty-four hours—the meeting on the dock. The first kiss. Standing in the doorway of the donut shop. Holding Jade in my arms on the shore of the lake.

"Dinner's ready." My mom's voice brought me back to the present. I took a deep breath, walked to the bathroom, and washed my hands.

"There's the stranger," a jovial voice of greeting from my dad as I sat down at the table with the family. "Whatcha been up to the last two days?"

* * *

After dinner, I made my way out to the barn to catch up on my chores. I stepped out the back door and was immediately greeted by Whitie. She always seemed to know when I was around. She nudged me softly with her forehead. I squatted down and gave her a pat on the head. She turned and rubbed her side against my body.

"Nice to see you old lady," I said as I gave her a hug around her neck. She turned and slowly walked away. I stood up and made my way into the barn. Jeffy had his head lowered into his feed trough quietly gnawing on his dinner. My parents' horses were on the other side of the barn, resting in their stalls. I picked up a pitchfork and began moving hay into piles. It was my job to keep the barn clean and while my dad did some of the work while I was gone, I had about two hours of work ahead of me before I could relax for the night.

When I emerged from the barn, the sun was halfway hidden by the hills on the opposite side of the lake, the faint outline of a half-moon was visible high overhead, and the light from the receding sun colored a few puffy clouds in the sky.

I walked across the yard and plopped onto the hammock. It swung evenly from side to side, slowed, and came to a stop. I placed my hands behind my head, crossed my outstretched legs and stared up into the emerging galaxy of twinkling lights. The familiar sound of the Cicadas mating call began to bounce off the trees and echo through the hills. It was comforting, as I knew nothing else, growing up in my hidden lake town.

I drifted off to sleep in this comfort zone. A short nap at the end of the day always brought peace of mind. It brought with it a sense of safety, laying in the backyard, protected by the invisible bubble that seemed to have been placed around our family stead. Nothing could disturb me here. Yet, the day's events ran through my head, Jade, Tim and Tanya, our sightseeing tour through town and around the lake trails. And, even though I lay there in comfort, the incident, just about twelve hours ago, flashed into my head, and sat there.

I wasn't sure if I was dreaming or if I was awake—thinking. I saw the people sitting at their tables staring at me as I stood in the doorway of the donut shop chastising them, Jody standing behind the counter, looking at me with a scowl. I heard my words over in my head. My heart rate quickened. I could feel a rhythmic thud in my chest. My unencumbered rest was done.

I took a deep breath. I sat up. I blinked twice, a third time, and then stood up. I walked over to the chicken coop and leaned my forehead against the door. I looked in through the slats. They were asleep on their roost. Their calmness drew me back to my center. My heart rate slowed.

A few more deep breaths and I was back to my normal self. Anger was not a usual part of my makeup. Yes, I had been frustrated at times. Yes, I had had conflicts with my sisters or felt angry with my parents once in a while. But today was different. My anger took on a life of its own, something I had never experienced before.

As I stood there, I heard the creek of the backdoor and footsteps. I turned. My dad was walking my way. He was partially blocking the light over the door, creating a halo around his body.

"Hey, bud. What's going on?"

"Just checking on my friends out here. Hadn't seen 'em in a couple days."

"I'm sure they missed you," he said sincerely. I chuckled in reply. "Sounds like you had an eventful couple days," he added.

"Uh-huh."

"You wanna tell me about the girls you guys met?"

I paused for a moment... "Not much to say."

"Well, it seemed like you had more to say this evening, so I wanted to give you a chance."

My dad walked over near the barn and picked up two old wooden chairs. He brought them back over and set them down. "Take a load off."

We sat down.

"You know," my dad's voice broke the silence. "Your mom and I were talking yesterday... about how quickly time has gone... about you entering high school. Man, hard to believe—you looking forward to it?"

"Yeah, I think so. I mean, how much different can it be? Really just moving to a couple different classrooms."

"True. But it's a new stage in your life. You'll be thinking about your future. You'll be thinking about where you want to go, what you want to do, who you want to be—what type of man you want to be."

I looked to the sky and let out a guttural "Hmmm..."

"In fact," he continued, "you're probably making decisions now that affect the type of person you will be. I mean, you may be making decisions on purpose or even without knowing it that will affect who you become."

"I'm sure."

"So, you sure you don't have something more you wanna talk

65

about?" Silence. "What about the girls you and Tim met?" My dad said with a slight smile. I wasn't sure if he was inquiring about boy-girl things or something more. He's never talked to me about girls much, but maybe that was because I never showed much interest in girls other than Lily, and my secret lust for Lily was sealed deep inside me... and Tim.

"Nah. We just hung out. Nothing big."

"Okay." He looked at me sideways. A few moments later he stood up and began to walk away. He took a few steps, stopped, turned, and said, calmly, "We got a call this morning about something that happened at the donut shop."

Again, silence.

I stood slowly and turned away from him. "I don't think I'll be going there again."

"I would think not. At least for a while." The quiet night hung over us.

I turned, "Dad?"

"Huh?"

"You know that family that bought the property next to us."

"Yes."

"What type of people are they?"

"They seemed nice to me. I met the husband and wife last fall when they were checking out the land. And then the Realtor brought the wife by earlier this summer to ask a few questions."

"Well, that's the girl I met at the beach."

"Right. They told me they had a daughter about your age. I think she'll be going to the high school next year."

"Yup." I turned and looked at him. "Well, I was holding her hand when we went to the donut shop this morning and the people didn't like it."

"What did they do?

"Just stared at us, but Jody asked us to eat outside."

"Huh?"

"I didn't get why until we got outside." I paused. Even sitting there, talking to my dad, my heart began pounding again. "And then I couldn't control myself. Tim was angry. Jade was crying. So I just ran inside and let them have it."

He sat back down. "Huh, interesting." He nodded.

"Who called you?"

"Logan."

Logan was a friend of my dad's. They did carpentry work together off and on. He lived with his family on the trail between our house and Tim's. We usually went to his house for summer corn husking. Their other family comes from the east side of the lake and we all join in the picking and husking for a day. It's worth it because right before the sun goes down Logan throws a couple huge pots of corn onto the fire and my dad cooks Venison he's been storing up from the fall. Last year I brought Lily with me. I think that's when I really knew I liked her. We sat near the fire with corn all over our faces and hands. That seems like a long time ago now.

"How'd he find out about it?"

"He said he entered when you were at the counter."

"Oh, I didn't see him."

"Yeah, he let me know what happened. Are you Okay?"

"I think so."

"Do you want to talk about it?"

"I mean, I'm fine now. But angry at the same time. I really didn't know what to do."

"It sounds to me like you took care of it on your end."

"As best I could. I really like her."

"Like I said, her parents seemed nice. I don't know much

about 'em except for they come from down south. I'm sure we will get to know 'em when they settle in."

"What I don't get is why they care who I'm with."

"You mean the people at the donut shop?" He paused, shook his head, and let out a sigh. "Some people just don't like people who are different."

"What's it matter?"

"It doesn't. It don't matter a damn thing."

"What would you have done?"

"I'm really not sure. But I'm also not sure I could have kept my cool. But no matter, it sounds like you did what you needed to do."

"I tried."

"You did more than that. You stood up for your friend and that's the right thing in my book."

"I'm glad Tim was there. If he wasn't, I don't think I would have had the courage to do anything."

"Tim's a good kid. I'm glad he was with you, too."

We stood there in silence for a couple minutes. A few bats darted low above our heads and the Cicadas nightly mating call danced with the darkened sky.

"And by the way," my dad said as he put his hand on my shoulder, "I hope you didn't learn all them bad words from me." He reached up and tussled my hair. I looked up and smiled. "Yup, Logan told me everything..." a slight laugh escaped his mouth. We walked inside, shut the door, and were immediately engulfed by the scent of Mom's fresh bread. "I think it's time for bed. We got some good eats to look forward to in the morning," he said as he reached to the ceiling and yawned. I'll see you bright and early in the barn. You still got some chores to catch up on."

I turned toward my room, but hesitated. "Dad," I called down the hall.

He stopped without turning. "Yeah."

"What did Logan think about what I did?" From behind I could see his head tilt a little and could sense his mind turning over.

"He said I raised a good kid." He turned and paused briefly. "Well, his actual words? 'He's a tough little shit.'"

Chapter Seven

The rain was pouring. My sweats were soaked and muddy and my once white running shoes were an off-color of gray. My feet pounded through the puddles on the trail. My arms swung in cadence as I leaned forward to gain momentum to keep up with the pack. It was mid-fall, four months since high school graduation. It was week nine of the season and it had been a difficult beginning to my freshman year of college. Two-a-days in the heat of late summer, training with some of the best runners in the surrounding states, and now a grueling run up Cardiac Hill in the falling rain.

Little did I know that Tim's brief interest in joining the high school cross-country team would lead us in a new direction. We spent the next four years training and competing around the state. We also didn't know that the new runner who moved into our small lake town was a girl. She was the one who, just by reputation, drew the attention of the coach and the few athletes in our small town.

During that time, our team did well. We climbed up the ranks each year. Our boy's team placed tenth at the state meet my junior year and fourth my senior year. And I found something I loved. Well, two things actually. I placed twenty-fifth at the state meet my junior year and third my senior year. Running became one of my two obsessions. The other was the new girl runner who moved into town. And, she is what fueled my obsession for cross-country.

After Jade and her family set up their trailer on the property next door, I went over early each morning and we would go for a run. She introduced me to the sport that first summer we met when I visited her in cabin #3 one day. She told me she had to keep her training up and if we wanted to spend time together I could join her. I asked her what she was training for. When she told me cross-country, I immediately said, "So you're the runner the guys were talking about?"

"What do you mean," she asked.

"A couple guys tried to talk me and Tim into joining the cross-country team because some new kid moved to town that was pretty good."

"Well, huh? Whatcha think?" She looked at me with a smile.

And that was it. I mean, not quite it. That first year she ran me into the ground. I had to work my ass off just to keep within ten feet of her for a couple miles and then when I fell off she went a couple more.

Jade came in ranked pretty high in the 13-14 year old division in our state. She won a couple big races in middle school and was poised to make the jump to high school. When she told me she wasn't sure about moving to our small town, it wasn't just because of the possible racial tension, but also because her goal was to win a high school state title, and not the little one that she would have to enter with our team. But, as her dad told her, times don't lie, so she changed her focus from winning state to having the best time, in all divisions. And that is what she did. Twice. She placed fifth in small school state her freshman year, second her sophomore year, then never looked back.

We ran almost every day. It became what we did. Sometimes when we trained, we ran the horse trails and met Tim halfway and the three of us would end up at one of our places for the night. But, almost without fail, Jade and I met each other between our houses and ran, mile after mile. And it led me to that rainy day my freshman year of college, on that trail, doing everything I could to keep up with the gliding feet of seasoned runners.

We were on what they called "Cardiac Hill." The trail circled around the outskirts of campus and led to a dirt hill that seemed, without warning, to go straight up into the clouds. It took me two years before I could run up Cardiac Hill without bear-crawling the second half. But on that day in mid-October, I had no such luck. And until I could continue running up Cardiac on two feet, I figured I had no chance of cracking the varsity line-up. It looked hopeless for me and the two other freshmen who lived at the tail end of this fourteen-man squad.

The rain continued to fall and bounding feet in front of me sent mud in my direction, hitting me in the face, arms, and legs. After just a few weeks it became my goal to stay as close as I could to the back of the lead pack and as far in front of the other two freshmen as I could—which was my only consolation at that point.

It was tempting, at first, to join the other freshmen because misery loves company, and it was miserable running behind the lead pack. But, I fought the temptation and so far had achieved at least that one small goal.

The trail turned left and just like always tried to fool me by starting with a gradual incline. I pushed any feeling of joy I felt as the slight pitch carried me forward, knowing that soon I would be hit by a climb straight up to parts unknown. And just a few strides later, like a wall of mud, there it was. My legs were already tired and my heart was beating fast, yet I kept my eyes on the group in front of me as they quickly spread apart, the faster runners taking off, and even the slower runners increasing their distance from me and my fellow freshmen.

My feet kept moving, or so I thought. They felt like they were moving, but I also felt I was not going anywhere. I pumped my arms. I lifted my knees. I chipped away at the slippery slope with every labored step. Groans bellowed from deep within my gut, yet I kept my eyes up and willed myself on.

I slipped. I caught my balance. I did everything I could to keep my hands from touching the ground. I chanted the one mantra that got me through all the strenuous miles of training, a mantra that emerged the first time I felt fire in my belly, that drove me to confront the evils of racism in the donut shop—"You're a tough little shit." Those simple words got me through many miles, burning legs, burning lungs. Those words helped me climb high on the podium at the state tournament in high school and I used them to compel me as I struggled as a young collegiate athlete.

But, this was a different story. This was a new level. Everyone on this team had climbed high on the podium in high school. Everyone here had their own mantra that helped them tear through the miles, work through the pain. It was my job now to see, not only if I could compete with them, but first if I could survive.

"You're a tough little shit," I continued as I slipped, stumbled, and crawled my way to the top. My feet moved. My feet slid. Halfway up, my hands touched the ground. I bear crawled a few feet. I ran a few more. I slipped and fell and got back up. And finally, I made it to the top.

Rain pelted my head. It ran down my face. It obscured the visual field in front of me. I squinted my eyes to find the group ahead of me. Off in the distance, I saw the last of the group disappear around the bend up ahead. My body had once been trained to follow and later had learned to lead. But now, at this new level, I had come full circle and had to summon what once was a driving force to grow as a runner—not just to follow, but to latch onto, to pull myself in, and to catch. I had to learn again, to use the invisible rope my high school coach taught me to carry when I ran, the one he told me to use to lasso the runner in front and pull myself in. But, at this point, I had neither the strength nor the wherewithal to pull the rope from my belt. I had just enough left within me to finish—and at that point, my main goal was simply to stay in front of the other two freshmen.

I kept moving. I brought the back of my hand to my face and wiped the muddy rain from my eyes, rounded the next bend, ready to join the lead pack on the track. They were staying warm, jogging slowly in a group when I rounded the corner and down a set of stairs, and then through the gate near the track. A chant from the group began. They applauded. They hooped. They hollered. The upperclassman cheered me on to finish.

"Hoot, Hoot, Hoot," they chanted and clapped their hands. "Come on freshman, bring it in..." My feet motored faster and faster until I felt like I was sprinting a 100-yard dash.

I slowed down, joined the group, and turned just in time to see the other two freshmen come into view. "Hoot, Hoot, Hoot..." I joined in the melee, bringing the other freshmen to the finish.

* * *

That night I lay on my bed in my dorm room, alone. My roommates, both athletes at the school, were out. Phil was a freshman basketball player. Much like me, he was fighting to survive and find his way on court. They had just started to rev up their workouts as their competitive season was still a few weeks away. He was at the second of two-a-day workouts. He left the room a short time ago with a bit of a pep talk from me, much like the pep talk he gave me the day before. We learned quickly that sticking together would make things much more tolerable. Chris was on the soccer team. He was a sophomore starter—a phenom most would say. He was the second-leading scorer on the team, right behind a fifth-year senior. They were in the dead center of their season and were off on a week-long road trip. Lying in the darkened room with nothing but a small desk lamp illuminating the corner, my body ached, yet, strangely enough, I felt okay.

Over my first two months in college, I created a schedule for myself wrapped around workouts, meals, classes, and studying. It didn't allow for much extra rest, apart from the six to seven hours of sleep I got each night. So, lying there was a treat. It felt like the ice cream my mom scooped onto her warm apple pie. My sisters and I would spend mid-day after our chores stirring the cold mix until it became hardened. We would carry the sweet concoction into the kitchen and be overtaken by the smell of warm, cinnamon apples cooking in the oven. Later we would scarf down our dinner as fast as we could in anticipation of the sweet dessert. Mom would cut extra-large slices and plop a heaping scoop of homemade vanilla on top. No matter how full we were from the main course, we always made sure to lick every last morsel from our plates.

The ice cream comfort I felt as I lay motionless would not be long-lived. I turned over and set my alarm clock so I wouldn't miss study table in an hour. I closed my eyes, relaxed my body, and drifted off.

Chapter Eight

Climbing the stairs to the third story of the library usually seemed a pretty simple task, but these days, trudging to the study carols to meet with my team after a long day of classes and practice had become an arduous task. Tired legs, along with a tired mind, made each stair a hurdle in itself. This became a part of my daily routine twice a week and as much as I didn't look forward to the climb, this gathered study time saved me that first year. Learning study habits and having the support of teammates and tutors was the reason I was able to stay eligible.

After an evening of studying, a meal, and a night's sleep, mornings came quickly. Twice a week I had early morning classes. I would drag myself out of bed, grab a bite to eat at a campus cafe by my Biology 101 class, and then sit, as attentive as possible, in the middle of 200 freshmen, hurriedly scribbling down notes and equations in my binder.

"Hey, freshman." I heard one morning as I was leaving my Biology class, my head reeling from the morning's lesson. I turned to see Thomas, one of the top runners on our team.

"Hey, Thomas," I called back. I was a bit surprised. None of the older guys really paid any attention to the freshman outside practice.

"You want to join me at the pub? I'm meeting a couple of the other guys there in a few minutes." The pub was a campus bar and deli where lots of students hung out between classes.

I could skip my morning in the library, I told myself. "Sure, I've got an hour till my next class."

He smiled and slapped me on the back.

We walked in uncomfortable silence for a few minutes. I wanted to start a conversation, but I really didn't know what to say.

"When you start runnin'?" Thomas finally asked.

"Ninth grade. Actually, the summer before I started high school."

"You look pretty good out there. At least from what I can see from up front." He laughed. I couldn't tell if he was being genuine or if he was giving me shit, but I decided to take it as a compliment because I needed all the positives I could get. "Yeah, well, we didn't all start at the front." He added. "I mean, you know Donny came in with the right motor. But me, I was draggin' ass when I was in your shoes." I kept my gaze forward, not knowing how to respond.

We entered the pub and found a group of tables at the side. We tossed our backpacks under the tables and sat down. Tommy swiveled his head around, surveying the inhabitants. He cocked his head to see around a group of people and waved his hand in the air. "Yo, Petey. Over here," he bellowed across the room.

We were joined by Petey, and then a few minutes later Donny, and finally Jeff. I sat there quietly listening and observing—complaints about classes and professors—inquiries about a date Jeff had been on the night before—talk about the upcoming meet. Finally, Petey turned to me. "What you up to?" I looked at him and shrugged. "How you gettin' along?" He added.

"I think I'm making it." I smirked.

"That's how I felt when I was a freshman," Tommy added.

"You run hard... for a little runt," Donny said, half paying attention to a ruckus at the other side of the pub. "Muther-fuckers..." he mumbled to himself as he scowled toward the commotion.

I turned to see what he was referring to. Two guys were standing tall and obscuring a group of people at a table in the corner. "What's going on?" I asked.

"They can't leave them well enough alone," Donny replied.

"Can't leave who alone?" I craned my neck to see who was sitting at the corner table, but couldn't see who it was.

"Ain't none of our business," Jeff concluded.

"Yeah, but it bugs the shit out of me," Donny added. He took a deep breath and brought his attention back to our conversation. He turned to me, the scowl still pasted on his face, "You run hard, but if you think you gonna take any of our spots, we'll run you into the ground."

I turned my head and closed my eyes and then I looked back at him. I wanted to stand up to Donny, whose attention was now back on the table in the corner, still blocked by the tall guys. I wanted to hit him with, "Bring it on" or maybe something even stronger, but I was afraid if I did, he would actually bring it on and at this point, I was doing all I could already. So, I sat there like the freshman I was and watched as the others at my table wove in and out of conversation.

A little while later, I looked at my watch. It was about time to head to class. I noticed the noise had died down in the corner, so I peered over hoping to see who was there. Two black guys sat, engaged in a quiet, but intense conversation. I recognized one of them. He was a friend of my roommate. Both were freshmen on the basketball team. Phil brought him by our dorm a few days ago before practice.

I felt a lump in my throat as I turned to leave. I didn't have to wonder what had happened. The two tall guys were obviously mad and they were also white. Flashbacks of home. Flashbacks of Jade. My memory was quickly filled with incidents that plagued her time in our small town.

"See you guys at practice," I said to the group who were not at all paying attention to me. Still, I gave a quick wave and walked out.

* * *

I made the Pub a new stop in my morning routine and got to know the guys a bit more, twice a week sitting at a table with the older runners after my Biology class. While I was welcome, I was still the freshman. I was part of the group, but not fully integrated. I would sit quietly most of the time and listen, once in a while getting a word into the conversation. "Yeah that was a brutal run" or "Yup, she's good looking" I would add if one of the guys was nice enough to ask, "Whatcha think freshman?"

A couple weeks after my first visit to the pub, another ruckus broke out as I sat with the other guys in our usual spot. I stood up and leaned to the side so I could see around a crowd of people that had gathered at the back.

"Whaddya see?" Petey asked.

"Hold on. I can't see anything." I stepped around some chairs and then weaved through the crowd. A minute later I was back with my group.

"So?" Donny asked with haste.

"Looks like two guys are picking on a couple people sitting at one of the tables in the back."

Donny stood up, hands on his hips, and shot a glare toward the crowd. "Picking on who?"

I groaned. Memories flashed through my mind. "A black guy and the girl he's sitting with."

"What are they saying?"

"They were telling them to get out."

"Motherfuckers..." Donny fumed. He pushed his chair aside and shoved his way through the crowd. I stood up and quickly followed. Four other runners fell in line behind me. I caught up to Donny. He was standing near the table, silently watching. I stood next to him, shoulder to shoulder.

"Hey, boy... I told you to get out," a tall, well-built white guy yelled at the two seated at the table. No reaction. The bully leaned down, placed both hands on the table, and growled, "I'm not going to say it again." He took a deep breath, "Get out."

My blood was suddenly hot, my mind filled with memories. The donut shop and the staring eyes—a school dance when Jade and I were physically pushed off the floor and I was called a nigger lover—looking into Jade's tear-filled eyes on numerous occasions after she was bullied or threatened—hearing the comments about the colored girl when Jade was receiving her awards at the state championships.

"Get up," the white guy yelled. Still, the two stayed seated. "I said, get..." He was cut off in mid-sentence as I found myself standing between the table and the bully, looking him square in the face. I wasn't sure how I got there, yet I felt the surge of energy that overtook me at the donut shop that first time and stood my ground. "What's up, little shit?" He put his hands on me and tried to push me out of the way. I stood my ground. My vision narrowed. I saw nothing, but the racist bastard in front of me.

"Knock it off," I said with all the manhood I could muster. I stepped forward. Less than an inch separated us.

"This doesn't concern you. Get the fuck out of the way." I'm sure he was yelling at me, but for some reason, I heard only a whisper.

I lifted my chin so my eyes were looking directly into his. "I'm not moving." I took another step forward, bumping my body into his, forcing him backward.

He reached out, extended both arms, his palms landed flat on my chest. I stumbled back, my ass hitting the table behind me. I didn't say a word and walked back into his space.

He looked bewildered.

I took a deep breath and shook my head.

He turned around, shoved his way through the crowd, and was gone. His friend followed behind.

I stood there for a moment, which seemed like an eternity at the time, and then turned to see the upperclassmen—Donny, Thomas, Petey, and Jeff—talking amongst themselves, but keeping a clear eye on me at the same time. It was a different look than they had ever given me before. It was as if they now saw me for the first time.

They walked up to me as the crowd dispersed. "Dumbass," Jeff said with a hint of laughter. He shot me a grin. Thomas put his arm around my shoulder and we started to walk away. I took a quick peek over my shoulder at the table where the two were sitting, but the table was empty.

Chapter Nine

The next week the varsity runners were gone for four days at a quad meet, running against the top three teams in our conference. They took eight runners on the trip and left six of us with our assistant coach for training. He was a ball buster and expected from us the same commitment and grit shown by the older runners. Since we didn't have a race that week, he took it upon himself to make up for that. He was a member of a running club and set up a mock race for that Saturday. We would match up against a few of the master-level runners in our area.

The varsity was gone Wednesday through Saturday, so he scheduled a practice race on Wednesday—three laps on the 2,500-meter trail loop we used for home meets—and then a four-lap race against the men from his club on Saturday.

The Wednesday practice run went well. I finished fourth out of six, ahead of the other freshmen, but closer to the runner ahead of me than usual. In fact, with a kick at the end, I ended just two seconds behind third place which was about a half minute better than normal. And, I finally had an inkling of hope. With the right mindset, I may be able to overtake the third and maybe the second runner. There was still quite a gap to catch the lead runner, but with hope and a nickel, who knows?

At the end of Wednesday's practice, we set out on hill intervals.

Coach wanted us to run the distance of lap four at a higher stress level so we were able to have a good kick at the end of Saturday's race. Thursday and Friday we had mid and low-intensity workouts to taper for the race, training as if we were preparing for the quad meet the varsity was in.

Coach took us through the same nighttime and pre-race routine we would follow if we were on the road trip. He talked to us about day before carb-loading all the way through sleep, morning wake-up, meals, and warm-up. He told us that three of the varsity runners were graduating at the end of the year and someone had to take their place. "It might as well be you, " he made a point of saying. When practice was done on Friday, he led us in a visualization session, walking us through a varsity meet, the pressure, the competition, pushing through the finish. He wanted us to see ourselves running, representing the team, facing obstacles, prevailing at the end. "Remember how this feels," he said. "Take this feeling with you tomorrow during the race."

* * *

I woke up earlier than usual on Saturday. Something about what Coach said excited me. The muddy runs up Cardiac Hill, the struggle to finish sprint workouts, lying in bed at night, body aching, all seemed worth it now. I had a goal in my head, to take one of those varsity spots next year. But today, I had to run down at least one of the guys in front of me, one of the three that might prevent me from being a part of the varsity team as a sophomore.

It was five-thirty AM. I was standing, back to the door, looking out the window of the communal kitchen in our dorm, shared by all students on the third floor. It was still dark, save for a few lights that illuminated the path to the main part of campus. A rabbit hopped into view, under the light and paused.

"Morning," a soft voice broke the silence.

I turned, "Hey." It was Shelby. She lived in the room at the end of the hall.

"What are you doing up so early?" She inquired.

"We have a practice race this morning."

"Ah," she smiled. "Well, good luck. I just came in to make some tea."

"Thanks." I turned back to the window. The rabbit was gone. *Hmmm*, I said to myself.

Water ran in the sink. The slow fill of a kettle gurgled. Clicking of knobs on the stove echoed against the concrete walls of the room. I turned back. Shelby was sitting at a table reading a book. I walked over to the sink. My breakfast dishes sat, filled with water, soaking. A few flakes of oatmeal floated about. I rinsed and dried my dishes and placed them in the cupboard labeled with my name. "Well, okay. I gotta finish getting ready. Talk to you later."

"Yup, hope the weather holds out for yuh," she replied. I smiled and nodded.

I made my way down the hall to my room. Phil and Chris were both snoring away, resting soundly, making sure to sleep as long as possible before they woke and made their way to morning workouts. I did my part not to disturb them. I put my racing shoes in a plastic bag before placing them next to my clothes and towel in my duffel. I grabbed my track top and rain jacket and put them both on snugly. I zipped my bag shut and threw the long strap diagonally over my head and across my chest. I checked my watch—six-ten, and then out the door I went.

I walked down the darkened hallway. For some reason, it seemed I was preparing for more than a practice, more than a trial race against a few unnamed runners. It felt like I finally had a shot to move up, to prove myself. Maybe it was because I didn't have to contend with the varsity guys. But, at that moment, it really didn't matter. I felt good and was going to take it seriously.

I made my way down three flights of stairs, to the dorm lobby, and pushed through the double glass doors that opened onto the courtyard between the cement-gray dorm buildings. A slight mist met my face and hands. I turned the corner onto the path and walked the ten minutes to the track.

I was the first one there. The field lights cast just enough glow to see the first three lanes of the track that circled the field. We were to meet at seven o'clock, so I had a few minutes before anyone would start showing up. I set my bag down under a covered tent on the field at the edge of the track. Under cover of the tent, I sat on a bench, pulled my race shoes out of my duffel, and removed them from the plastic bag. I removed my shoes from my feet and replaced them with my race shoes. I wiggled my feet into the snug runners, first the left, then the right. I tied each of them in turn and then stood up, bouncing up and down on my toes and then took a few steps to make sure they were tightened to my liking. When I was satisfied, I squatted down on one knee, double-knotted the first shoe, switched knees and double-knotted the other.

I stood up and walked out from under the tent. I stepped onto the track and walked slowly down lane one for ten strides. I turned around and strode back, softly lifting high knees into the air, one and then the other, opposite arms swinging to extend my strides. I continued my private warm-up, bounding backward, then skipping forward, and then jogging halfway around the track. I stopped on the far side and walked across the field back toward the tent. Off in the distance, I saw two teammates making their way down the stairs from the parking lot toward the track.

Light began to faintly show in the sky. Three shades of gray clouds began to emerge. The mist in the air, still palpable, added an ominous glow under the field lights. As the team started to gather—two, then one, then one more, then the coach, then the final member—we circled up together under the tent. Coach reviewed the schedule and prepared us for the nine AM start.

By eight-thirty we were jogging slowly toward the starting line. We finished our individual warm-ups with race starts, striding down the beginning of the course a few meters, turning and jogging back to the start, repeated three times.

Our opposition began to gather near the start. Seven men, of varying ages and skill levels. Coach introduced us. We shook hands and exchanged pleasantries. "Five minutes 'till start," Coach bellowed into the air. He smiled.

I walked near the start and grabbed a water bottle from the team gear bag. I swished a mouthful of water around, leaned to my left and spat it onto the ground, filled my mouth again and swallowed. I took a deep breath, held it, and let it out slowly.

"Okay, gentleman, approach the starting line." Coach instructed. "Two minutes to race time."

Unlike a normal meet, there was plenty of room to find a good position. I positioned myself to the far right, on the inside shoulder of one of the older men. He looked my way, "Good luck." He reached over and patted me on the back.

"You too," I muttered, my eyes trained on the path before me.

"Thirty seconds…" Silence. "Take your mark…" Pause. The gun sounded and we were off. Feet pounded. Bodies nudged to and fro battling for position.

I started hard, pushing to find a way into the front pack. The course began wide enough for at least six runners to pass, but quickly turned a corner through the trees and narrowed. I fought to stay in the front group and challenged myself to fight for position as the course narrowed about 200 meters in. After bumping shoulders, I found myself side by side with one of the older men, pinned on the right, directly behind Petey and Donovan, who both had spent time on varsity earlier in the season when a couple of our lead runners were nursing injuries.

The leaders sped up and put distance between me and my older partner. I kept my eyes ahead of me, but still noticed the man next to me was running with relative ease. His gait was smooth and relaxed, his breathing inaudible.

We reached the red flag, halfway marker for lap one. Petey had moved ahead, with Donovan not far behind. I felt comfortable and was still within maybe twenty meters of the leaders.

As we approached the end of lap one, I heard soft, rhythmic footsteps approaching. I wanted to turn and see who was coming, but forced myself to keep my focus. The course widened and the footsteps were suddenly on my right and now in front of me. One of the older men passed me with little effort and caught up with the leaders. My first lap partner decided he had had enough and took off as well, leaving me alone.

We passed the red flag again and finished lap two. I was sitting fifth and could clearly see the group ahead of me, now led by the two older runners, followed by Petey and Donovan.

Red flag number three. I had to figure out how I was going to approach the final lap. I hadn't been this close to the front pack since last year in high school. I quieted my mind, listened to my heartbeat, and slowed my breathing. The course led to the right, so I glanced over my right shoulder. No one was within fifty meters. I turned my focus back to the front pack.

I decided to work on cutting the distance in half. I wanted to be within striking distance of the lead the next time the red flag was in view. I sped up, elongated my stride, and pumped my arms with more force. I threw my imaginary lasso and began to pull myself closer to the lead group.

You're a tough little shit. My mantra echoed in my head. *You're a tough little shit... You're a tough little shit.* I felt gravity pulling me forward. I felt my legs bounding across the earth with ease. My arms pumped, my lungs opened, my mind knew nothing but what was in front of me.

Lap three completed. The trail opened up. I surged forward. I glided over the ground. My feet barely touching down. The group ahead of me was spreading out, two falling behind, two fighting for the lead. I could see the red flag ahead of me about 200 meters.

The trail weaved one way, then the other. I sped up a bit more, feeling my legs in a way I had never felt them before. They were unattached, yet they were still a part of me, still under my command. I willed them faster. The distance between me and my teammates was shrinking. Soon, I was on their heels, but they blocked my way around. As we passed the flag Petey began to fall off. I seized the moment and squeezed in front of him and alongside Donovan. He shot me a glance and grimaced.

I lifted my eyes to the runners ahead of us, one man in the lead, another just a few meters behind him. We passed the red flag for the last time—1,200 meters to the finish. I continued pumping and began leaving my teammates behind. I could almost touch the man in front of me—800 meters to go. He gave me a quick look over his shoulder, took a deep breath, and sped up, but I kept with him, shoulder to shoulder—400 meters. My stride got stronger and I moved ahead, one man between me and the finish—200 meters. I continued to close the gap, squinted my eyes, and pushed forward at breakneck speed.

I turned the final bend. The finish came into view—150 meters. For the first time, I strained. I willed myself to catch the lead runner. My chest heaved. My legs turned—50 meters-40-30-20... I leaped across the finish, a few paces behind the winner, Old Man #1. I stumbled, but caught my balance.

Hands on my hips, I walked forward. I took a deep breath and I turned to see the next runner cross the finish, Old Man #2, and a minute later Donovan, and then Petey.

I greeted my teammates with high fives, "Good job guys," I said instinctively.

They both looked at me with confusion. "Uhhh, yeah. You too," Donovan replied.

"What got into you, Freshman," Petey chided, between breaths. I chuckled, not yet totally aware of the height of my accomplishment.

The remainder of the runners finished over the next few minutes and we gathered for a warm-down, jogging down the course about a half mile and back.

We walked to the track, quietly. Wet sun rays peeked through parting clouds—slices of gray-blue fighting to be seen.

"Good run today," Old Man #2 sidled up next to me.

I turned and smiled, "Thanks."

"I didn't expect that kick."

"Actually, me either," I replied with a small laugh.

"Keep it up. I'll be looking for your name in the paper soon."

"Yeah, thanks," I replied. He reached out, shook my hand, and turned to another conversation.

I cocked my head and looked at the sky. I turned to see the other two freshmen walking together, quietly—everyone else walking in somewhat of a makeshift circle around Coach.

We met at the tent and sat together on the ground, young and old. Coach recapped the race. He explained that the man who won was an All-American ten years ago and is currently running professionally. "And he took it a bit easy on you guys today," Coach chuckled. I looked across the tent at Old Man #1, feeling pleased, yet wondering how easy he took it on us. By the end of the race, my legs were going as fast as they could. They were working at full capacity. *How much more did he have in his tank? Could I find more in mine?*

The meeting ended. I gathered my stuff and said goodbye to my teammates. The tent emptied quickly. I stood outside on the track, zipping up my jacket. Coach called my name. I turned as he walked up to me. "You ran well today," he said.

"Thanks."

"Your time today puts you ahead of the alternate spot."

"Well, yeah. I figured I must be close."

"You're right there with the number seven spot." I stood silently. "We have an outside shot at qualifying a full team for Nationals in two weeks. We'll be making decisions on who gives us the best shot. Six and seven aren't set in stone at this point.

"Okay. Cool," I said awkwardly, not really knowing how to respond.

"You mind sharing with me what was different today."

"What do you mean?"

"Well, you shaved just under four minutes off your time."

"I'm not quite sure. I mean, I just took it seriously. I never really knew I had a shot at varsity this year, but today I told myself to let loose."

"You think you can do it again?"

"I'm sure I can."

"Make sure to rest your legs tonight and go for a slow two to three-mile jog in the morning. Work the lactic acid out of your muscles before Monday's practice."

"Yeah, for sure."

"I'm going to be talking to Coach Jay tomorrow. He's been looking for someone he can count on in the final two spots. I'm sure he'll have his eye on you in practice next week."

"Thanks," I replied with unusual confidence. I threw my bag over my shoulder and turned to head home. I wanted to shout to the birds in the sky as I walked up the stairs to the sidewalk that led to the dorms, but I caught myself in time and kept my cool—at least on the outside.

Chapter Ten

Monday came and went—classes, practice, study table, dinner. Tuesday, much of the same. I stayed away from the pub and actually hadn't been back since the incident over a week ago. Wednesday was a long day. We had an early morning workout and ended the day with a fundraising event to raise money for the athletic department. I worked hard in practice to stay up with the varsity runners, at least the last couple. I had a newfound confidence that helped me run free, to push myself further... but I was a bit anxious because Coach Jay had not talked to me all week. He ran practice as usual and I couldn't tell any difference. *Was he watching me? Was my effort being noticed?*

Thursday was a different story. I ran into Thomas after class and he asked why I hadn't been to the pub lately. I told him I'd been busy studying, but I'm sure he saw through me. Ever since I confronted that racist prick I wanted to stay clear.

"Come on. Join us today."

"Sure," I replied, tentatively.

I spent Thursday and Friday in the pub with the guys. Conversations mingled with music piped in through speakers in the ceiling as we sat in our group sharing stories and talking about girls. While everything was pretty much normal, for me it had changed. I was now a part of the conversation. I was no longer alone in the group. I was included. No one said anything different. They didn't mention how I stood up to the guy in the back of the pub. They didn't bring up my newfound confidence on the trails. They just included me.

It was a bit awkward at first. I didn't know how to be a part of the conversation. I sat there thinking of what to say, but it just didn't come. The upperclassmen made it work somehow, without effort. I'm not sure if it was conscious or it just happened, but little things pulled me in, closer to the group. They would turn and look at me when they were talking. Someone told a joke and slapped me on the back as they burst out laughing—and this time, not at the freshman's expense.

By the time we were leaving the pub on Friday, I had worked my way in. I had found ways to interject myself into the chatter. I had added my comments, my opinions, and they heard me.

As we got up to leave, Donny swung his arm around my shoulder. "What the fuck got into you the other day."

"Whatdya mean?" I asked.

"Why'd you stand up to that punk?"

"Oh. Um... I just don't like that shit."

"Yeah, but what made you do it?"

"I don't know." I paused, took a breath, and slowly shook my head.

"Well, something's changed. You're not the same little freshman you were before."

We stood there for a few moments in silence. Then, I ended up telling him about Jade—about how we met and the struggles she had, and we had had together, as a mixed couple. I told him how she introduced me to running and how we spent our four years together on trails and at races. I told him how, even though she was the best female runner in the state, it didn't matter, there

93

were still troubles, and because of that, after graduation, she decided to move away and go to an all-black university.

We made our way outside the pub and sat on a bench in the quad. The rest of the guys had left while he sat quietly and listened.

"It was difficult. But I understood why she had to go."

We sat there for a couple minutes. Neither of us knew what to do next. Finally, he looked at me. "How'd you leave it? I mean, are you guys still together?"

I nodded my head. "Yeah, we're still together. At least that's what we talked about before we left for college. I've only talked to her a couple times since then, though."

He paused and let out a small sigh, "Well, you've got running to focus on and you seem to know how to stand up for yourself. I think you'll make it alright."

It was nice to have someone to talk to, at least for the moment. I wasn't sure if this was a one-time thing or if we were friends now. But, it didn't matter at that point.

* * *

I ran with even more confidence that afternoon. I felt lighter and more relaxed. I easily kept up with the last few varsity guys, passing them toward the end of our four-mile workout, coming in just behind the top four runners on the team. I no longer looked over my shoulder to see where the other freshmen were. In my eyes, I had solidified my spot among the top runners on the team.

On Saturday, we met at a trail off campus that wound around two small man-made lakes. We were going to do three timed laps with a ten-minute rest period in between. A figure eight around the two was just about 2,400 meters. Coach Jay told us our goal was to run hard each lap and get faster each time.

We spent the first ten minutes warming up on our own and then Coach broke us up into two groups to do our laps. For the first time, I was specifically set with the varsity. No explanation. No fanfare. He split up the groups, set us on the starting line, and off we went.

I had no time to adjust my thinking. I didn't know if I had been moved to varsity or if this was a trial. So, I just took off running. I had to work hard, but felt pretty good the first lap and kept up with the group. Lap two was a bit different. I wasn't ready for the change in intensity. This was not a normal second lap in a race. We had a ten-minute recovery period and the lap started out in an almost dead sprint. I fell behind quickly and never caught back up.

I walked off by myself to recover for the final lap. I felt like I blew my chance and I realized that this lap would be even faster than lap two. *You're a tough little shit,* I repeated to myself, three times. I slowly walked back to the group as everyone began gathering at the starting line. I told myself to start fast and keep up with Donny as long as I could. Donny had blown everyone out of the water the last lap and I was determined to stay as close to him as possible this time.

We stepped to the line and took off. I stayed with him stride for stride for 1,200 meters. He moved ahead just a bit, but I picked up my pace and followed closely. I was his shadow and was connected to him. I heard footsteps behind me, but I could tell they were far enough away that I didn't have to worry. We approached the final 400 meters and Donny began his push. I quickened my feet and kept my shadowlike connection, right behind him. We got closer to the finish and Donny began to increase his lead. I tried to stay connected, but I was the shadow no more.

I continued to run hard through the end and crossed the line second, about twenty-five meters behind Donny. I redeemed my second lap flop and, tired as I was, I felt good.

At the end of practice, Coach Jay talked with us about the final week leading to Regionals and about our chance to qualify a full team to Nationals—we were ranked third and the top two teams automatically qualified to move on. He then announced the seven varsity runners. I sat there, focused on his voice, eyes closed—Donny, Jimmy, Thomas, Ben, and then... and then I must have gone into shock. I heard my name, but it didn't register. I was announced fifth ahead of the final two varsity runners. *Coach, would you repeat that please,* I was compelled to say. But I just sat there, eyes closed, and listened to the final two names called.

* * *

Regionals was a blast. It was my first long road trip with the team. We were gone for four days. Thirty teams and over two hundred runners ran that day. We finished ten points behind the second-place team, just missing out on qualifying our entire squad. I had the run of my life and a week later, when the runners selection was complete, I was headed with Donny, Jimmy, and Thomas to Nationals. I had gone from a freshman, hanging on by a thread, just a few weeks before, to a national qualifier. And, just a year ago, I was running trails around my small lake town with Jade and Tim. It was a whirlwind. Now, in just two weeks, I would be competing against the best college runners in the country.

* * *

I thought Regionals was fun, but Nationals was on a totally different level. Almost 260 runners from across the country lined up for the start of the race. It was the nicest course I had ever seen. It was like running on a Golf course. A wide-open 600-meter, green grass start, meticulously groomed, led to a two-mile expanse of sprawling lawn that wound through evergreens. The mid-morning sun brightened the trails and shown through dappled shade and groves of trees. The remainder of the race wound through hard-packed dirt and grass until the final 200 meters was like running on the eighteenth green at Pebble Beach.

I finished in the top half of the race, crossing the finish line a couple minutes ahead of Thomas and just a minute and a half behind Donny. I was on a new plane, finishing third on my team by the end of the season, something that I never knew possible when I stepped on the college campus for the first time back in August.

Not long ago, I had no goals beyond trying to survive practice. Now, I have a taste of what's possible. After the finish, I felt good. In fact, I felt like I had more to give. I knew I didn't give everything I had, but I never knew I had more, before today. *What could I have done if I really let myself go?*

Suddenly, I felt a pang of regret. I knew I had just lost this chance to see what I could really do. It was gone and I would have to wait for a year to again line up against the nation's best. I watched the individual and team awards being handed out and celebrated. Cheers rang through the crowd. Elation gleamed on the All-Americans' faces. I wanted to see what they were feeling. I wanted to see what I had to shoot for.

All of a sudden my regret turned to anger. I felt it well up inside me. I felt my face turning red. I wanted to scream. I wanted to take off and run, run as far and as fast as I could. I wanted to prove to myself then and there that I had more, and that I could compete at the top. It was that moment, watching trophies hoisted overheads, that everything changed.

* * *

I woke up early the next morning in the hotel bed. I glanced at my watch, we were heading back to school in a little while. I jumped to my feet, eager to begin my ascent. I pulled on my shoes, a pair of shorts, a T-shirt, and my warm-up jacket.

Thomas rolled over, half asleep. "What time is it?"

"About five-thirty."

"What yuh doing up so early?"

"I'm going for a run. I'll be back in a little while."

He sat up. Shook his head. "'Wait. What?"

"Don't worry. I'll be back soon." I bolted out the door and headed down the walk and onto the pavement outside. I started with a short walk and worked into a slow jog. I picked up the pace and pushed hard. The anger that I felt yesterday had subsided, but my determination had not.

The cool morning air felt good on my body. A light breeze accompanied me as I ran. Cars whizzed by on my right. I ran through evenly spaced lights on lamp posts overhead, moving briskly down the sidewalk. I counted twelve paces between each light, then ten as my feet moved faster. A park appeared up ahead. I ran to my left, onto a dirt path that led into and around the perimeter of a baseball field and then onto the grass where I pictured families having picnics and throwing Frisbees. I made a loop to the entrance of the park and onto the side and headed back to the hotel. I counted nine and then eight strides between lights. The hotel was in sight. I picked up my pace to an almost sprint, kept the pace up for two blocks, and then slowed. When I reached the parking lot I walked and made my way back to my room.

Thirty minutes later, drenched in sweat, I sat on the end of my bed, undid my laces and lay back, feet still touching the floor. Thomas was still under the covers in the opposite bed. I lay there feeling my heart through my chest. Drops of sweat ran down from my forehead, passed my earlobes, and onto my neck. The base of my back was wet, and my underwear was sticking to my legs. I took a few deep breaths and waited for my heart rate to slow.

I stood up, lay on the floor, propped my feet up on the bed, and let the blood run through my body. *This is day number one*, I thought, *364 more to go.*

* * *

Over the next nine months, I entered a number of road races anywhere from 5K-10K. It didn't matter how big the races were, I just wanted to run. The first one I entered was our local Turkey Trot 5K race, the Friday after Thanksgiving. There were maybe 150 runners from elementary kids to grandparents. It didn't matter to me though. I entered and ran, and finished far ahead of everyone.

I entered the Spring 10K in a town about forty-five minutes from campus. I was surprised how many good runners were there, nothing at the level I was trying to reach, but at least they gave me a bit of a push through the first part of the race.

I decided to stay at school for the summer semester to continue training and use the college facilities. I took a full load of classes so that I would have a reason to stay organized and focused. I kept my early morning training schedule as if we were in the preseason, went to classes during the day, and worked out in the late afternoon.

I entered my third race in the early summer, a popular 10K in the heart of the state capitol. It was then I realized I needed to set specific time goals prior to racing. I never knew who was going to show up at each race. It may be somewhat competitive or it may be more recreational, so it wasn't good enough to just win a race. I had to work on specific areas of my running, setting PRs was generally good, but each course was different so a time on one course may not equate to a specific time on another course. For example, on this particular run, I bested my 10K PR by over a minute, but after looking back, the course had nothing to offer outside of distance. So, I began looking up course information— difficulty, previous course records, weather predictions. This helped me gauge the race and gave me an idea about specific goals for each race.

Three weeks later, I ran a 10K held at one of the colleges in our conference. It was a challenging course, lots of hills, a couple of tight turns along a steep incline, and there were three runners who placed ahead of me at Nationals. I ended up placing third, besting two of the guys who beat me at both regionals and Nationals, but also forty-five seconds slower than my PR. An example of when time didn't matter. I had to look at other factors to measure my performance. In this case, the rigor of the course and beating quality competition was the important part.

I continued training and racing through the summer, hitting

two more 10Ks before taking a needed rest headed into my sophomore season. A total of five races and almost nine months of hard work and I was feeling primed and ready for a breakout season. Two weeks later it was time to join the team for the first day of preseason. Last year, on this same day, I was nervous and didn't know what to expect. In contrast, this year, I didn't feel overly emotional, one way or the other. I just felt ready, like it was time. I woke up early on the first day of my sophomore season and continued what I had done all spring and summer.

I had seen a couple of the guys over the summer, but most had gone home and we hadn't seen each other for a few months. There was chatter among the group, the usual excitement that came with a new season, and when Donny, now a senior, came in with the grace and confidence he always had, every one turned and looked. But I wasn't surprised by his entrance and it didn't intimidate me like it did last year. I had grown physically and emotionally and now felt like an equal.

I walked up to him, stuck out my hand, "What's up Donny?"

"Hey, you're looking good. I heard you were training all summer," he replied.

"Yup. Spent my time hittin' the books and keepin' in shape."

"Good. Maybe I'll have a bit of competition on the team this year," he winked and nodded his head. But Little did he know, that wink was all it took. My fire was lit and as the season progressed, Donny and I formed a strong one-two punch, pushing each other at practice and later in competitions. He was still a step or two in front of me when push came to shove, but I knew I wasn't far behind.

While we were a team of fourteen runners, a group of seven on race days, and five scores at the end of each competition, it was almost like the others were an afterthought. Donny and I made each other better. We were always minutes ahead of the next guy on the squad. Halfway through the season, Coach Jay told us that he had never had two guys feed off each other the way we did.

After four competitions, we had placed in the top ten in each one, including placing one-two in a tri-meet against two teams ranked sixth and eighth in the nation. It was shaping up to be the season I had envisioned.

In mid-October, we lined up against our in-state rivals. We were ranked second in our conference and they were ranked sixth. We knew if we ran the way we were capable we would take the top four spots in the race with relative ease. So, Donny and I decided to push each other further than usual. It was a three-lap course. We would switch off leading the first and second laps, and then let it all out on the final lap.

The race started fast. I led lap one at a blistering pace. I had never run this well before. I heard Donny breathe, in and out, his feet hitting the hard-packed dirt, right behind me. As we rounded the corner, back to the start, I slid over to the right, giving Donny just enough space to take the lead. He picked up the pace and passed me. I took a deep breath and urged my legs to go faster, drafting in his wake.

We approached the end of lap two. Donny moved to the right, offering me a place beside him. I matched his pace, stride for stride. I could feel his energy and I used it. His power was my power. Halfway through lap three, out of nowhere, *You're a tough little shit.* The words rang in my head. Instinctively, my feet moved faster. My arms churned with more force. I began to move ahead. Donny picked it up and moved past me. I made another move, caught and passed Donny again. He continued the back and forth and took a three-stride lead.

You're a tough little shit, I told myself as I made one last push. Two-hundred meters to the finish. I pulled ahead and increased the distance until I was a good twenty meters in front. I crossed the line, stumbled, caught my balance, and walked to the side, watching as Donny finished, slowed, and dropped to his hands and knees.

The fire was raging. My blood was pumping. I looked on as Donny struggled to his feet. *This is my team*, I said to myself.

* * *

I was the top runner on our team heading into Regionals. Donny and I were still working together, but our roles had changed. No spoken words needed. No ritual passing of the torch. I just stepped in front and took the lead and he could do nothing about it. My legs felt strong. My mind was focused.

I placed second at Regionals. Donny took third and we qualified our entire team for Nationals—the first time in school history. On day 362 of my year-long trek back to Nationals, our team loaded up into a van and we drove six hours to our destination.

It was a successful weekend. I placed in the top thirty, continuing my improvement. Donny and I ran a majority of the race together, just as we had been doing the last half of the season. At the end, he couldn't keep up with my kick and I crossed the line three places in front of him. While it was a massive improvement, and the third-best finish in school history, I was not satisfied.

As I stood, watching trophies hoisted above heads for the second time, I had a new feeling inside me. There was no wonder, no guessing what I could have done if I had given it my all. I knew I had given everything. I knew I had nothing left at the end. This year the difference was, I also knew I had to find another level and I was sure I had it in me somewhere. I just had to find it.

Day 365 complete... Day one begins tomorrow.

Chapter Eleven

Winter break came and went quickly this year. I had become accustomed to living in a new world, a world far from the lake where I grew up. I was not compelled to go home like most of my friends and teammates. I missed my family, but I was driven by a new force. I did spend three days with my family during the holidays, but I was restless the entire time. Jade's family was not home for Christmas, Tim spent the time with his grandparents on the other side of the state, and Lily was engaged to a guy she met in college and was with his family for the week. Everyone I knew was spread out across the country doing their own thing and that's what I wanted to be doing.

As the Winter semester started in January and classes kicked off, I threw myself, full throttle, into my studies and training. I kicked my training up a notch, adding weight training three times a week in the mornings. I could feel my strength increasing daily and was visibly stronger. I made it part of my spring training to run Cardiac Hill once a week and I was now able to make it up with relative ease. My once skinny self, stumbling and straining to make it to the top was now an afterthought.

Late in the Spring, after one of my regular morning workouts, I showered, dressed, and headed to class. As I walked through the quad I glanced at my watch and realized I had time to stop by the Pub and pick up a sandwich.

I entered the open doors, looked through the crowd, and saw Thomas sitting with a girl at a small table near the bar. He looked up and saw me. I waved. He smiled and motioned for me to join them. I grabbed a sandwich and drink and, just as I was headed to their table, yelling erupted behind me. I turned to see two tall white guys cornering a black guy by the entrance.

I set my food on the table in front of Thomas, turned, and slowly made my way toward the entrance. Flashes of high school bombarded my mind. I heard myself yelling at the people in the donut shop. I saw myself stepping in front of Jade as a group of kids was harassing her after she won a race. I took a deep breath and tried to control the heat flowing inside me, the anger that enveloped me just as it did when I realized why people were staring at me and Jade.

I paused, just behind the two harassers. I listen to their anger. I listened to their bigotry. I watched as they put hands-on, then pushed, yelled, and laughed at the young man.

I shook my head and I closed my eyes briefly, trying to figure out what to do and wondering why no one else was doing anything.

Quietly, a voice spoke from behind me. "Be careful." I turned. Thomas, standing off my right shoulder, had a serious look on his face.

I turned back. The bullying continued. A few onlookers gathered.

I pursed my lips, furrowed my brow, and took a couple steps closer.

Words shot from the bullies to the victim put an end to my spectator role, "Fuckin' darkies. Get the hell out of here," one of them growled.

I moved up beside the tormentors and turned to face them. "Knock it off and move on," I said with a loud booming voice.

"Ain't none of your business."

I took a step closer, now within arm's distance. "Sure is... You guys are disturbing my lunch."

"If this fucker would leave, everything would be just fine," one of the bigots pointed to the victim.

I raised my eyebrows, leaned forward, and looked directly into both their eyes. "You're the ones who need to leave," I said sternly.

They looked at each other and laughed. "You his mamma," one of them said.

"You heard him." Thomas had stepped up beside me. "Leave," he demanded.

We stood, strong and firm, staring them down.

"You guys are fucked up," one said. They pushed their way past us and stormed out the doors.

I turned to the victim, said nothing, and smiled. He smiled back. We nodded at each other and parted ways.

Thomas and I went back to his table. His friend was sitting there quietly. I glanced at my watch. I was late for class.

"You've got balls," Thomas said with a wink and a sense of admiration.

"Thanks for the backup," I replied. I grabbed my sandwich and drink. "I've gotta run. I'm late for class."

"See you later, big man."

* * *

A week later I was back at the Pub. I was sitting with a few guys from the team when I felt a tap on my shoulder. I turned to see the victim from last week.

"Can I have a word?" he asked.

"Sure," I replied quietly.

I followed him to the side of the room.

"My name's Joseph." We shook hands. I introduced myself. "I wanted to thank you for last week."

"Yeah. Anytime."

"Well, I also want to ask you not to step in next time."

"Whatdya mean?" I felt a look of confusion disrupt my face.

"I don't want to sound ungrateful, but we need to handle these things ourselves."

"Huh?" I said, perplexed.

"I know you meant well, but they gotta see we can take care of ourselves. Otherwise, they'll continue pushing us around."

"Ah, shit. I'm sorry."

"Don't need to apologize. Like I said, you meant well."

"Right. Hmmm..." I cleared my throat. We stood there for a few seconds, neither of us knowing quite what to do or say next.

I stuck out my hand. We shook, gave each other a silent smile and a nod, and he walked off. I stood there, thinking—wondering—trying to figure out what just transpired. I hadn't talked to Jade in a few months. She called me right after the start of Winter semester, but after I left the Pub that morning, I knew I had to give her a call.

* * *

That night, the phone rang and her roommate answered, "May I ask who's calling?"

"It's her boyfriend," I replied.

"Hold on. She's in the other room." I heard a muffled

conversation on the other end.

"Hey," A beautiful voice rang out. "I've been thinking about you."

"Oh, man. It's nice to hear your voice."

"It's been a while, huh?"

"Yeah. Haven't heard from you since January. Everything okay there?" I said. I could feel myself getting emotional.

"Pretty good. Just trying to get through midterms."

We talked for a few minutes as I tried to figure out how to explain what happened today. "Before you go, I wanted to ask you something."

"What's up?"

"Um, well, a week ago..." I explained how I stepped in between the bullies and who they were, or at least that they were white. And then I told her what Joseph said today.

"Ahhh. I see." She paused. "You know he's right, don't yuh?"

"I get it. It's—It's tough though. Just standing there."

"I know. I remember."

"What? You mean high school?"

"Yeah."

"Did you feel the same way?"

"Not exactly. I was glad you were there of course. And I loved how you stood up for me like I was your girl. But it didn't feel good that you had to help me because I'm black. I know you would have done it even if I wasn't, but the fact that I'm black makes it difficult and that always made me feel bad. And, even though I've grown past most of that, it still weighs on me sometimes. So, I see why it is important for us to fight our own battles."

I sat on the other end of the line, listening, trying to take it all in—trying to understand.

"You still there?" she asked after a moment.

"Hem.." I cleared my throat. "I'm here." Pause. "I'm sorry."

"Whatya sorry for?"

"I don't know."

"Don't be sorry. Just keep being yourself."

"How do I do that if I can't stand up to these guys... to the fuckin bastards."

"You're a good guy. You'll figure it out."

The conversation slowed and changed. We meandered in and out of a few random topics, but the weight of our sharing was still heavy.

"Hey, Jade. I miss you."

"I miss you too."

"I was thinkin' about trying to find a race near you somewhere and thought maybe we could meet up and run together."

"I hear you've become quite the runner. Not sure I can keep up with you anymore," she laughed.

"I'll wait for you at the finish."

"You better. But only if you win the damn thing." A jingle of sweetness floated through the receiver.

"Of course," I said with confidence.

"Okay. Let's find something after Winter quarter."

"I'm looking forward to it," I said, with newfound energy.

"Me, too," her soft voice comforted me as we ended the conversation and hung up the phone.

* * *

Jade was right. Over the last month of the semester, I saw Joseph a few more times at the Pub. We smiled and nodded, and once exchanged pleasantries. I felt awkward at first, but quickly was at ease. I still wondered what I would do if the bullshit returned, but I was at least cognizant of the role I needed to play at this point. I decided that, if nothing else, I had to be a witness.

Chapter Twelve

As March turned to April and April to May, school began to wind down, but my training amped up. I found two races to attend, one at the beginning of May, just across the border that usually attracted some nationally ranked senior-level runners, and then a race with Jade at the beginning of June.

The race in May was going to be a challenge, something I needed if I was going to take the next step. It was the biggest race I had ever entered—over 1,000 runners. They lined us up by expected mile time. I was near the front, but there were still at least a hundred runners ahead of me. I was both excited and nervous. It was a hot day, the ten AM sun was already overhead beating down on the crowd. Before the start, sweat was dripping down my back. Standing, waiting for the race to begin, it was like floating in a sea of people, waves rippling side to side, and the sea creatures were restless. I waited, bent over, with my hands on my knees, ready to bolt at the sound of the gun, but not sure how to get through the crowd. I stood up on my tip toes and looked around. I tried to move up to the next marker, but it was too late. I was caught in a pocket, people walling me in on each side.

A few minutes later, Beep... Beep... Bang... the race began and the sea churned. It was both frustrating and exhilarating. As the wave of people moved forward, I looked at the large black and yellow clock as I approached the start. It took me twenty-five seconds just to get to the starting line. I felt anxious. I had to figure out a way to make up the time, to catch up to the leaders—which ended up being a futile effort.

I did make up some time, passing dozens of people, but there were still quite a few runners who finished ahead of me. Overall though, I felt good, and I made a mental note to move to the front before the race began next time—a learning experience for sure.

A couple weeks later, before I left to meet up with Jade, I received a letter in the mail. I had placed first in my age division and was invited to a national road race in late July, something that had never even crossed my mind. In fact, I didn't know anything about it. The letter said that there would be runners from all across the country and a few select international runners from two different West African countries.

My first instinct was to call Jade, but I held off. I thought it would be a great surprise when I saw her the following week. Anyway, I had a bunch of studying to do before finals week began and had to stay focused on what was in front of me. My days were filled with classes and training and my nights with studying. I was struggling to understand my upper-level anatomy class and needed as much time in the library as possible. So, for the time being, I put Jade and the race out of my mind.

Cramming wasn't my favorite thing to do, but it was necessary, especially as I finished a few of my core courses and set my sights on a major in Kinesiology. I attacked it as I did my training, head-on and full bore. I didn't know any other way.

I was exhausted at the end of the two weeks of finals and felt a wave of relief as I laced up my shoes for a run after my last test of the semester. I told myself that today was a recovery run, even though I hadn't raced for a few weeks and had been training a bit lighter as my focus was elsewhere. I set out on a long, slow run—no destination—no time limit—just me, the sun in the sky, and the sound of my footsteps on the pavement.

As my day came to an end—sophomore year in the rearview mirror, recovery run complete—I lay on my bed and shut my eyes. I took a deep breath and let my mind wander. Jade's face was the first to appear. Her dark skin. Her bright smile. Her comforting laugh. I saw us together by the lake. I felt her hand in mine. I realized I was more excited to see her than I had let myself know. We spent little time together the last two years. In fact, we had only seen each other twice, once during our freshman year spring break back at the lake and second at a meet this past season. Our teams were at the same race, but female runners ran the day before the men. Luckily my team arrived before her team left and we had an hour together. It was strange, and rushed, as we had just enough time to exchange pleasantries before she was back with her team and gone.

I woke up the next morning and called Jade to finalize our plans. I was hopping on the bus in two days and taking the six-hour ride that would reunite us. We would have ten days together, the first five filled with training and our scheduled road race and the final five would be spent at the nearby beach. I was excited and hadn't looked forward to anything this much in a long time. Everything in my life had been so intense it was nice to have something outside college life and competition to look forward to. I enjoyed my last two years, in fact, I relished the growth, the competition, the unified focus it took to perform at a high level. But the emotions I felt as I heard Jade's voice on the other end of the phone were calming and made the stresses of college life melt away.

* * *

As the bus pulled up, I felt a longing. I was still half asleep, standing in the dark morning, and wanted the next six hours to fly by. I looked down at my feet and my two bags, taking mental note of their contents, double-checking in my mind to make sure I had everything I needed. Bag one, training and racing. Bag two, beach and leisure. I ran through the items I remembered stuffing into each. I knelt down, unzipped bag one, and ran my hands through its contents. Everything was there, including my lucky socks. While I was not particularly superstitious, as some athletes are, I did feel more comfortable with my feet snug in my lucky socks on race day.

I zipped up bag one, patted it softly for good measure and, still squatting down, looked up at the bus, waiting for the door to open and beckon me to enter and begin my trip.

When the doors opened, I stood up, one bag in each hand, and watched a few passengers trail off and then I approached and mounted the stairs. The coach was about half full, people scattered with no rhyme or reason throughout. I walked down the aisle and found two open seats next to each other, three-quarters of the way back. I plopped my bags in the aisle seat and sidled into the other.

The bus sat idle for a few minutes before the doors closed and the motor roared to life. I looked out the window and the skies that were dark at my arrival were waking. I looked at my watch and added six hours. I should arrive by eleven o'clock.

I sat back, closed my eyes, and ran my right hand along the armrest until I felt the little silver button. I pressed and felt my seat slowly lay back a few inches. I scootched my body from side to side and settled in for the ride.

A quick woosh filled the vestibule as the air brake was released and the rumble of the engine intensified. My seat rattled as the bus backed up, turned, and leapt forward onto the deserted morning street. I turned my head, peered out the window, and watched sleeping buildings pass by. I could feel heat flow at my feet as the revving engine blew air through the floor vents. My eyes felt heavy and I allowed them to slowly close and my mind to drift away.

As the bus motored on I sat with my eyes shut, feeling asleep, yet aware of my surroundings. The slight shaking of the cabin was comforting. A sudden jerk and woosh of the air brakes jarred me awake. We had stopped. It was fully light outside now and I could see a few people lined up with bags outside the bus. I peered at my watch, in an instant it was eight-thirty. We were more than halfway there.

The bus driver came on the loudspeaker, "We have a ten-minute stop. You may go inside to use the facilities or get something to eat. Our scheduled departure time is eight forty-two. Please be in your seats and ready to go by that time."

I stood up and made my way up the aisle, down the steps, and out the door. I walked a few paces from the bus, reached for the sky, stretched my body, and yawned. I squatted down and stood back up and then bounced in place a few times. I closed my eyes and lifted my chin to the sky. The warm sun hit my face and a light breeze wafted through my hair.

I opened my eyes and walked into the unknown bus depot. The bathroom was off to the left, in a corner next to a waiting area of chairs and small tables. I walked in, relieved myself, and washed my hands and face in the metal basin on the wall. I went back outside and waited by the bus until passengers began reboarding.

After I took my seat, I glanced at my watch. There were just under two and a half hours left on my trip. I leaned back in my chair, feeling a bit more rested than when I first sat down a few hours ago. And suddenly, I was jarred awake from a sleep I didn't know I had succumb. A tinny voice rang over my head, "We will be arriving at our final destination in approximately fifteen minutes. Thank you for choosing Greyhound as your travel companion."

I slowly opened my eyes and looked out the window. Blue skies and soft white clouds hovered over fields of baled hay. My heart was calm, yet my mind was full. The bus continued down the thoroughfare. I was soon to be reunited with the person who changed the trajectory of my life. The chance meeting on the dock at the beach in my small lake town, the day I finally had the courage to start a conversation, replayed in my head. Horse rides around the trails. Running those same trails as I learned the craft, as I learned my physical capabilities, as I got to know the young woman who would give me the strength and ability to run, not only the race, but the challenges that life put in front of me. Never before had I stood up to the challenges others presented, in a competitive realm or when called by social wrongdoing. She was my inspiration, she taught me what I had within myself, not by any purposeful choice, but just by being who she is.

When we ran the trails in the early days of our relationship I found myself chasing the beauty in front of me. I had to run fast and hard to keep up and finally was able to do so as an invisible force pulled me along. And then, as I ran ahead, she continued to push, and if I wanted to continue in the lead, I had to push even harder. That is where my drive was born, developed, and took shape.

We were connected. I felt it from day one, standing in the doorway of the donut shop, chastising the figures of hatred inside. I did not know what compelled me to do something I had never done before, but as time went by it was clear—it was my attraction and my love for the beautiful Jade. While my love may not have been fully formed or realized on that initial day, it was well on its way to taking hold of my entire being. During those first couple of years, there was never a single moment I told myself that I loved her. Early on there was never a single moment one of us said it to the other. It was felt—it was known—without words.

I turned from the window. I closed my eyes and took a deep breath. The bus pulled off the freeway and into town, made a few turns, and drove for a couple miles next to a train track. This small college town was built around and for the students. As we made the final turn onto the main street, coffee shops and bistros lined the sidewalks. Youthful faces sat at outside tables, sipping beverages, taking in rays of sunshine that lighted the pre-afternoon day.

We pulled into a large, open parking lot. A few cars were parked in front of a small, brick building. And there she was, wearing a pair of old cut-offs, and a white tank top. She seemed to glow in the sun. She stood next to another young woman, who I figured was the friend who would join us in the race. My heart pounded. I suddenly became nervous. I was never nervous around Jade, but our two-year separation was suddenly weighing heavy and I wasn't sure what to do or what to say.

The bus rolled slowly to a stop, air brakes swooshed, the doors opened. "Thanks again for choosing Greyhound," the voice echoed. I stood up and grabbed my bags and made my way out and onto the warm pavement.

I paused and looked her way. She smiled. A sudden feeling of calm swept over me. We were together, and all was right in the world, and I could feel it from head to toe.

I dropped my bags and we walked toward each other. We met, and I wrapped my arms around her. We said nothing.

She took my hand and softly pulled me toward her friend. "This is Kim," she said with a smile.

"And you must be the guy Jade has been talking about for the past two years," Kim replied.

"Well, I hope so," I laughed. I reached over and encircled Jade with both arms in disbelief that she was actually within arm's distance. We stood there for a few minutes. I shared my travel stories. Jade told me a bit about our plans for the day—lunch at her favorite coffee shop and, by my request, a run around the small lake by the college.

"Let's go get you settled in." Jade tugged on my arm and motioned me toward the car. A ten-minute drive in Kim's Toyota and we were at our destination, a small rancher with a brick facade and a large window overlooking the front yard. Jade and Kim rented out the basement suite which contained two bedrooms, a bath, and a makeshift kitchen and living room. It was located on the edge of campus and just a five-minute walk from the lake.

Jade and I spent the next hour side by side on the couch. She rested her head on my shoulder while we relaxed, for the first time alone, as adults. We talked periodically, but mostly just took in the moment. It felt good to be together after all this time. I closed my eyes and felt her in my arms. I leaned my head on the back of the couch and allowed myself to drift off, but not too far, always aware of her presence, her soft skin, her smell.

"So, we got this race on Saturday, huh?" She said in a soft voice.

"Yup. You up for it?" I replied, eyes closed, head still resting on the back of the couch.

"I'm sure I can handle it."

I took a deep breath and opened my eyes. "How's your training going?"

"Pretty good. Two short and three long runs a week. But nothing hard right now. What about you?"

"I had to back off a bit during finals, but made sure to keep up the mileage. I'll need to get a couple hard weeks of training in after this because I have a big race at the end of the month, but this weekend should be fun."

"Oh, where's the race?"

"California. There will be a number of world level runners there." I told her about the race I ran and the letter I received afterwards. She was excited and told me she would have to push me a bit harder now that I'm such a big shot.

"Kim is going to work out with us the next couple of days, but she said she would leave us alone today," Jade laughed. "So, we will make today fun and then I'll make sure you're working hard after that." She smiled.

We were finally able to get ourselves off the couch and off to lunch. We walked to the coffee shop down the road, sat on the patio with a couple sandwiches and cold drinks, and allowed ourselves to get reacquainted. We talked about our studies, experiences on the road competing and training, and our plans for the upcoming school year.

"Kinesiology sounds interesting," Jade said. Responding to my remark about my recent major declaration. "I've been thinking about education. Maybe teaching high school.

"That'd be cool."

"Ya, I've enjoyed my English classes, so I thought I would focus on that while I get my teaching certification."

"Sounds like you have got a good plan."

"I think I would enjoy coaching cross country, too."

"Well, you're good at it. You taught me how to run."

"I just ran while you chased me," she shot me a smile with her eyes.

"Whatever you did, it worked."

"I guess it did. You seem to be doing okay." Another jab, another smile, reminded me why I loved her.

I shook my head and smiled back.

After a few minutes of silence, Jade looked deep into my eyes... "What do you want to do after college?"

I pursed my lips. "I haven't thought much beyond my major... and running." She smiled and patted my hand. I could tell she knew I wasn't totally being honest, but at this point, I didn't know how to express what I wanted.

An hour later we were sitting in her backyard lacing up our running shoes. We set out on our first run together since the summer before we left for college. We started with a short walk and then picked up the pace to a soft run. We then ran three easy laps around the lake, about three miles, and a fourth brisk lap, before I took off for a final lap at race pace. When I finished, Jade led me to a field near the stadium on campus with a nice incline at the back end. We ran a few sprints up the incline and warmed down with a walk back to the lake and a quick swim to a dock about fifty yards from shore. As we held to the side of the dock, and let the cool water relax our bodies, I was drawn back to our dock back home.

"This is what I want," I said.

"What's that?"

"This is what I want," I said with a bit more confidence.

"Swimming. You want to go swimming?" Her sarcasm drew me deeper.

"Yes, I want to go swimming."

"Well, that's a plan, I guess."

"Yeah, I want to go swimming with you. It's how we met. On the beach. And then the dock. This is how it should be, forever"

"What are you saying?"

I closed my eyes. "I can see us. How we were in high school—on our lake. In our small town." I opened my eyes and looked at her. That is what I want."

"You want to be back in that small town?"

"No, it doesn't matter where we're at. I just want to be swimming with you, for the rest of our lives. Wherever that is."

"Oh... I see." She closed her eyes and breathed softly.

"I know we've never talked about our future. We've just been together. But, this is what I want. You are what I want."

"I've had the same thoughts," Jade replied. "I always wondered what would have happened if I never moved—if I never met you that day on the beach." We floated there in silence.

"So, what should we do next?" I asked.

"We've done just fine so far."

"I know. But we have two more years."

"And we've made it this far."

"I know we have. But, I run because I ran toward you those first few weeks." I looked deep into her eyes. "I run because I followed you around every inch of trail, every path, every hill we could find." I smiled. "I wouldn't be who I am if it wasn't for you." I pulled her closer. "I didn't know this early on, but after a while, I knew that I wanted to get faster, to do better, to win each race because of you." She said nothing. "You're right." I continued. "We've made it this far. But I have bigger dreams. I want to continue to run. To continue to improve. To win races I've never won before. But I also want you in my life." I raised my eyes to the blue sky. She remained silent. "Can we make it through the next two years the same way?" Silence.

Finally, she said, "I'm tempted. " She paused. "I'm tempted because I want to be with you, too—to just do it. To leave what we have done for the past two years and be together. I want it with all my heart." We looked at each other silently. "But is that what is best? Will that help us get what we want in the long run?" She wrapped her arms around me.

Without knowing what else to say, we swam back to shore, found our shoes, and walked back home.

That night, we lay in bed. A silence filled the room. And that's all it was. Silence. No answers appeared from the darkened recesses of our minds. A long night, a restless night, but I was comforted by her presence and I, if nothing else, knew that's what I wanted.

The next three days we spent long mornings lying in bed and we sat in the sunny backyard and drank coffee before our daily workouts. I wanted to talk about our future, but no words came. Everything had always been so easy between us. Things just happened. But now, even though it seemed we wanted the same thing, I was uncertain how to move forward. Or, at least I didn't want to admit what the next step should be.

We each had goals of our own and before we could pursue our life together we had to spend the next two years apart as individuals. I knew that was right, but I was conflicted. My love for Jade, which up to this point had never been formally declared, was making our time together both thrilling, yet painstakingly difficult because I didn't want it to end.

So, I remained silent and pushed the future where it should be, into the future. I focused on our short time together and running, for running is what drove me and Jade is the fuel that made running possible. This all made sense to me, it had gotten me where I was at that point in my life and it was the logical path forward.

Kim joined us on our last three workouts. The three of us ran together for a ways and then I picked up the pace and pushed myself forward. We had the race on Saturday, but I also knew I had to prepare for the invite that was less than four weeks away. I could tell my intensity was not where it should be, but promised myself I would put two solid weeks of training in when I got back to campus.

Saturday came and went. It was a small 10K with mainly local runners. A few former college runners were scattered throughout, but nothing at the level I was used to. From the start I hit a good pace and then hit my stride at the 5K mark. When I was done, it felt good waiting at the finish line for Jade and watching her glide through the finish. We rarely had ever run in the same actual race. I felt a joy seeing her and then Kim finish up. We were there together. I told myself I would remember this feeling, this is how I want running to feel. This is what I will use to carry me through the next two years.

We celebrated with a night on the town. We met Kim and her boyfriend at a local bar, danced, sang some Karaoke, and laughed. This was another rarity. I had not spent much time just enjoying myself. There was always some higher focus, something that made it difficult for me to let go and just have fun, but that night there was not a care in the world. We were together and we were happy.

Five days later, I was standing in the parking lot of the bus station. Everything I wanted— everything I needed—was there with me. I had my two bags, which contained my running gear and clothes, and Jade was there too. I held her tightly in my arms. We stood there silently as the mid-afternoon sun moved slowly across the sky. I closed my eyes, took in her fragrance, and imagined what it would feel like two years from now when I would not have to let her go anymore. I wanted to say something, but again, words escaped my tongue.

My thoughts were interrupted by a soft sputter off in the distance and I knew our time was coming to an end.

I held her tight.

The sound of the engine grew closer until I could feel the pavement jiggle under our feet, and the quick swoosh of the air brakes called out, "I'm here. Time to go."

I pulled her closer.

I felt her heartbeat on my chest.

"I guess this is it for a while," Jade said softly, tears welling up in her eyes.

I took a deep breath, paused—and then—and then slowly let her go and picked up my bags, the contents weighing me down as I walked backward a few steps and stopped. "Jade." My throat felt like it was closing. I couldn't speak. I shook my head softly. "Jade." I was frozen—"I love you."

She took a soft breath and smiled. "I love you, too."

Chapter Thirteen

The next two weeks went by quickly. Once I got back to campus, I threw myself back into training full bore. I put in eighty-five miles the first week, the most I had ever run in a seven day period. My days were filled with running, weight lifting, and physio, so I didn't have much time to miss Jade. While she was on my mind, running made me feel close to her, so that made it easier to lace up my shoes twice a day. I paired up with two of my teammates for training who were taking summer classes. While I did enjoy the solitude of running, the motivation of a training partner can not be overlooked and my teammates made the miles much more bearable.

I did everything I could to balance my training with race preparation, focusing on tapering at the right moment—allowing my body to recover and peak on competition day. I had never been involved in a race like this before and I was taking it seriously. The letter said that it was one in a series of three USATF invitational races throughout the year. If I did well enough, I would qualify for the next step. At this point, though, I wasn't concerned about the next step. I could hardly afford step one. In fact, when I got the letter, I was excited, but wasn't quite sure how I could afford it, so I brought it to Coach Jay. He offered for the club to pay my way, which was a godsend. He also helped me put together a training schedule, even helping me include the road race with Jade. He told me he would love to make the trip with me, but he was already part of a coaching delegation taking young runners on a European training tour in July. He did, however, put me in contact with a club coach he knew who would let me stay with him and would be my surrogate coach for the competition.

I was set.

* * *

On my last day of hard training, just seven days out from competition, I was returning from a long run. Coming down the steps and toward the track, I saw my assistant coach off in the distance, near the fieldhouse. He was standing with an older gentleman. As I rounded the track and made my way closer, I recognized the older man. I hadn't seen him since freshman year. It was Old Man #2. He was standing there with Coach, leaning up against the railing, looking over the track.

I jogged toward the fieldhouse and sat down on the edge of the track. A group of students were playing Ultimate Frisbee in the center of the field and a lone runner was making her way around the back side of the red rubber oval, the stretch of the track that ran along the edge of campus. I extended my legs out in front of me and reached my fingers to my toes. I paused and repeated the action several times. I took three deep breaths and closed my eyes, visualizing myself running smoothly along a familiar trail, a ritual I began about a year ago.

I stood back up and turned to look where my coach and Old Man #2 had been standing, but they were gone. I pursed my lips and gave myself an inquisitive, *Humph* and then walked into the fieldhouse for my daily physio.

Over the next few days, my body began to recover from the stresses of hard training. My lungs felt strong, and each day my body felt looser and lighter. Slow comfortable runs, coupled with physical therapy and rub downs, took all the lactic acid and tension out of my muscles. I had always enjoyed the last few days before a race—the way my body felt as it recovered and readied itself for competition. This time, though, the anticipation was heightened. I was excited in a way I had never been before.

I packed my bags and then double and triple-checked my gear to make sure everything was in its place. I sat on the side of my bed, nothing left to do. All preparations had been made. I always wanted to do well. I always wanted to win. But this time, my expectations were different. Do well, yes, but this time I was focused on competing with myself, doing what I could do to perform at my best. I had never raced against this level of competition before. I knew there would be some college guys in the race, but professionals and international runners were an unknown to me. I was excited, but didn't really know how to set my goals outside myself. I knew what I could do and I knew how to do it. And so, I decided that would be my focus. I wouldn't worry about my competition. I would run my race, from beginning to end.

A little while later I lay in bed, anticipating my flight the next morning. I would arrive forty-eight hours before race day, meet up with the contact my coach had given me, and scope out the course. But for now, I tossed and turned with anticipation for at least an hour before I drifted off to sleep.

Chapter Fourteen

The morning came swiftly and my heart pounded with excitement as I sat in the airport waiting for my flight. The sun was starting to lighten the sky as I looked down and checked the flight information on my ticket a second and then a third time. I had just enough time to buy a water and use the bathroom before boarding. I walked through the crowded concourse, bobbing and weaving through the people until I found the bathroom and then stood in line at a small coffee shop for a bottled water and a bagel. As the line inched forward, I pictured myself at the starting line waiting for the gun to sound.

"Sir? Excuse me. Sir?" The voice from behind the counter woke me from my dream. I walked the few steps to the counter. "Good morning. What can I get for you?"

With drink and food in hand, I sat at my gate, the last few minutes before boarding. I felt relaxed, yet the excitement still ran through my body. A voice on the loudspeaker beckoned me forward and to my flight. I stood up and walked toward the gate, imagining I was being summoned to the starting line of my next big race. I showed my ticket and walked through the doors and down the corridor toward the plane. I was greeted by the flight attendant and found my seat.

The flight took just over two hours and it was quickened by the book in my hand. When the call from the pilot announced our descent, I looked up from my book and peered out the window. Green fields sprawled across the ground. As I continued to watch, fields gave way to roads, and roads led to buildings. Toward the horizon, I could see the blue of the Pacific, spattered intermittently with small whitecaps that, from a distance, seemed to be frozen in place.

A deep hum vibrated underfoot as the landing gear deployed and soon the hull of the plane shook and bounced as it touched down. The plane taxied toward the gate and lights flashed on either side of the runway. Workers in yellow vests guided planes for takeoff.

"Thanks for flying United Airlines. We hope you choose us for your next destination."

I grabbed my bag from the compartment above my head and followed the line of people forward. I nodded to the flight attendant as I exited the plane and walked thirty yards up and out the corridor. A soft wind cooled my body as the corridor opened into the airport. I stopped and pulled a piece of paper out of my pocket and read the info—Baggage claim D/Mr. Jason Johnson, West Coast Elite Track Club.

I made my way to baggage claim and found a tall, lean, gray-haired man wearing a dark blue WC Elite Track T-shirt. I waved to him and he perked up.

"Coach Johnson?" I inquired.

"Yep." He stuck out his hand in greeting. "And you must be the young runner I've heard so much about."

"I guess so. I mean, I'm sure Coach Jay must have told you something."

"He told me you were his up and commer. You must be pretty good to qualify for this event." He shot me a smile and reached for one of my bags. "Let's head out. We can get to know each other on the road."

We walked out two large, sliding glass doors into the warm air. The throng of horns and revving engines caught me off guard. Yellow taxis swerved in and out. People waved hands and shouted for rides.

"This way." Coach Johnson motioned me along. I followed across a busy street, up a flight of stairs, and into a parking garage.

"How far away do you live?" I asked.

"About twenty minutes. And about forty-five minutes from the race. I'll take you down there in the morning to check out the course. I'm sure you want to get settled in first. Jay told me you'd probably want to go for a jog after lunch."

"Yeah, just an easy run. Nothing strenuous. Just want to run the travel out of my legs."

"I'm gonna meet a few runners from the track club at one o'clock if you're interested. One of our runners is in the race Saturday, too. We've been helping him get ready. You can use our training room at the college afterward if you want."

"That sounds good. I'll go for a twenty-minute jog before bed, too. If that's okay?"

"Of course. Whatever you need. There's a nice trail by my house. I'll tag along if you like. Unless you want to run alone."

"The company would be nice. I do most of my training alone in the summer since most of the team heads home. That's why I try to run a few road races after the season. I want to keep motivated."

"Ah, and that's how you qualified for this race."

"Yeah. I entered a big race downstate and then a couple weeks later I got a letter in the mail. I didn't think I ran very well because it was my first large-scale race and I started too far back and had to fight through the crowd."

"Well, good for you. Sounds like you've taken a lot of initiative."

"Coach Jay helped me design my off-season training and pay my way here."

"He's a good guy."

"He and my assistant coach have been really helpful."

"How long have you been running?"

"I started the summer before high school."

"I'll make sure you get what you need here. You're part of West Coast Track this weekend," he winked.

"Thanks. I appreciate it."

* * *

We arrived at his house and he showed me to my room. It was a modest home, decked out with running paraphernalia—pictures of what I presumed were Coach Johnson's teams throughout the years and a few trophies and other awards. I found an old picture that looked to be him running a race in college next to a framed letter from one of his coaches.

Sitting on a table beside the living room couch was a large, worn photo album. "Coach," I turned to where he was standing in the kitchen doorway looking toward me with a fatherly aura. "You mind if I take a look at your album?"

"Go for it." He smiled, turned, and vanished into the kitchen.

I picked it up with two hands, sat on the couch, and laid it on my lap. I opened the cover with a soft crackling of the plastic cover.

Old black and whites filled the first page. They looked like family portraits and a few candid shots of holiday parties. I saw what I thought was Coach Johnson as a boy, sitting with a big present in front of a Christmas tree, along with what I assumed were his siblings.

I flipped through page after page of happy moods, vacations, and birthdays, until one page caught my attention. A group of runners. Coach looked to be in high school. He was in the middle of the pack. Tall and lean, his face looked relaxed, his shoulder-length hair flying back behind him. The next page, a race bib stuck behind the sticky plastic—#1623—US Jr Nationals—the adjoining page, a red ribbon and a handwritten note with two words—Next Time. I flipped further through, he appeared again, exhausted, crossing the finish line. Handwritten in the picture's white border... Copenhagen, Denmark.

A few pages later, a newspaper clipping filled the page with a picture of three runners, stride for stride, leading a pack of runners just a few meters behind. The title read: "The Annual Beppu-Oita Marathon, Japan, Attracts Competition From Around The World." Scrawled at the bottom in red pen... "I will be there soon." A flip of the page and another race bib— #279—and above the number, a line of Japanese characters, which I assumed said Beppu-Oita.

Page after page, pictures of runners. Pictures of teams. Awards. Bibs. Toward the end, a wedding photo and a few pictures of babies and young kids.

I set the album back on the side table. "Coach," I said as I stood up and walked to the kitchen.

"Yup," he replied, setting down his teacup and looking up from a dog-eared book held in his left hand.

"So, I noticed you were married."

"Yes, long time ago."

"And you have kids?"

"Two. All grown up now."

"What happened to your wife?"

He closed his eyes and a soft smile appeared on his face. "She passed away a number of years ago." He cocked his head to the side and pursed his lips.

"Oh, sorry."

"Naw, it's Okay." He smiled softly. "It was rough and I still miss her, but life continues. And for me, she is always close by."

"How do you mean?"

"Well, we met each other running in college and we just connected. The miles we put in together gave us a special bond and, now, running makes me feel like she is right beside me."

I didn't really know how to respond. "Wow, interesting. That's nice," is all I could muster. I really wanted to tell him that it was the same for me and Jade, that when I run, even though we are hundreds of miles apart, running makes me feel connected to her. But my young love seemed too trivial.

"Say," Coach interjected as he looked down at his watch. "It's about time for us to meet up with the team for our afternoon run."

* * *

In a couple of car rides and some long conversations at his house, I learned that Coach Johnson was a 2x All-American in both track and cross country. He ran twelve marathons on four different continents. And he coached a successful youth track team. He shared some stories about how he and his wife supported each other's running obsessions throughout their twenties and he told me his kids found their own paths outside of running. His son spent a few years on a mission in South America before starting his own non-profit helping find job placements for immigrant adults. His daughter was married with children.

In a short time, I felt like I had known him for years. I told him about how I met Jade, some of the trouble she encountered as the only person of color in our small town, and how my love for her drew me to running. We talked about how we both felt closer to our girlfriend and his eventual wife through running—and how for both of us, running was made more important because of this connection. We had quite a bit in common, despite our thirty-five-year age difference. In some ways it felt like I was looking at an older version of myself. In fact, I was sort of hoping I was.

When we met up with a few of his runners for that first day's workout, it was quickly apparent that he had a great connection with them and I admired that. There were six runners, all college-age, four guys and two girls. We ran a brisk, forty-five minutes around the trails at a park in the middle of the city. It was one of the more enjoyable runs I'd had in a long time. It was just what I needed. No pressure—relaxed—good conversation getting to know other young dedicated runners.

At the end of the run, I took off with Geno, the other runner getting ready for the competition on Saturday. We pushed each other for the last ten minutes or so. We ended side by side, huffing and puffing, both with smiles on our faces. We slowed down to a walk, turned, gave each other a high five, and then walked back and met the rest of the group.

Coach Johnson, who was in his upper 50s, still ran with ease and looked comfortable trotting in with the others.

We spent the next hour stretching, chatting, and sharing stories. The six runners were members of the West Coast Track

Club, but came from three different colleges in the area. They asked me a lot of questions about where I came from since I was the new guy in the group. Most of them were from bigger cities and were interested to hear stories about running in my small lake town. They couldn't believe that my main transportation was either boat or horseback.

I still stay in contact with Geno all these years later and as adults we have met up a half dozen times to run in road races all over the country. And, we have backpacked the Sierra Nevada Mountains in California and the thirteen-mile Rim Trail in the Grand Canyon.

* * *

On the day of the race, I woke about five AM with a lump in my throat. I wasn't sure if I was nervous or excited, but I knew I was at least anxious. The race was at ten AM and we were scheduled to pick up Geno at eight.

I put on a pair of sweats and my flip-flops and went outside for some fresh air. Light was just beginning to show a dim blue in the sky. I sat on the front steps and took a deep breath. A faint salt smell was present in the air as Coach Johnson's house was just a few miles from the ocean. I stood up and walked a couple blocks around the neighborhood. Houses were spaced generously apart with mature evergreens between. The road was wide with sidewalks lining each side. A rooster woke the neighborhood in the distance, echoed by a dog in a nearby yard.

Race day forecast was mid-eighties at start time, rising near ninety by race's end. As I turned around and headed back to the house, I looked up to the sky. Not a cloud in sight and the dim blue had brightened to a soft powder blue. I looked at my watch, it was just after six.

I made it back to the house and went inside. The familiar scent of oatmeal wafted toward me and instinctively I anticipated my mom's voice calling the family to breakfast. A warmth filled my body and a metaphorical hug embraced me. I could see the smile on my mom's face as I entered the kitchen, my dad sitting at the long wooden table I helped him build when I was in sixth grade.

"Morning," Coach Johnson greeted me with a soft voice. I prepared your race-day oats.

"Ah, thanks. You remembered."

"Of course. I take care of my athletes," he smiled and winked in my direction. "How you feeling?"

"Good." I swung my arms in circles and jumped up and down a couple of times to mimic a pre-race warm-up. Then I threw a few slow punches toward the air in front of me.

Coach laughed. "Take a seat Rocky. Let's get you fueled up for the big day." It was nice being taken care of. I hadn't had that feeling, the feeling of being taken care of, since before I left home for college. I sat down at the island in the middle of the kitchen and he placed a steaming bowl of oatmeal in front of me and then poured me a glass of orange juice. "Everything the champion asked for," Coach said with a fatherly flair.

"Thanks. Just like I was back home at the lake."

"I aim to please," he quipped.

We spent the next little while meandering through breakfast. I thanked him for hosting me and treating me like one of his team. We exchanged some small talk before a lul in the conversation took hold. I sipped my orange juice and scraped the bottom of my bowl to get every last morsel, every ounce of energy into my body. The sound of my spoon against the glass bowl quietly echoed through the calm.

Finally, Coach broke the silence. "Whatcha looking for out there today?" We both paused. "What's your goal?"

"Well." I looked at my half-full glass of OJ. "Well." I looked up at Coach. "I've never competed in a race like this before. I don't have a feeling for what the top runners will be like. I've run a lot of 10K races, though. So, I've decided to focus on myself—on my race. I'm shooting to finish at or above my PR and I'll know halfway through if I am on track."

"That's a good start." He nodded his head and looked at me with a serious expression as if he was deep in thought. He smiled and then walked back and placed his empty cup in the sink. He stepped up to the island again and placed his hands on the counter, leaning toward me the slightest bit. "I watched you run the last couple days. I can see from the outside, what you have in you. My question to you is this, is a PR the thing that motivates you?"

"Yeah. I've learned over time that I have to compete against myself because there is not always another person to compete against who can keep up with me."

"That makes sense. But will that be the case today?"

"No. I'm sure the competition will be higher than I've ever experienced."

"Okay, good. In that case, what is it that drives you in a race that has the competition? In the middle of a race, what is it that keeps you moving forward, that quickens your pace, that drives you to do better?"

"The other runners," I answered.

"Good. So, while your goal is to PR, what will help you achieve that PR?"

"The other runners."

"Exactly. And would you be satisfied with a PR if you knew

that you still did not achieve the time you were capable of?"

I sat there and thought through the question.

Coach interrupted my thoughts. "Think about this. Do you know if you have come close to reaching your ultimate PR? Have you ever run your ultimate race?"

Deep in thought, I didn't answer.

"Maybe your PR is your PR because you have not pushed yourself to where you are capable of going. Maybe your PR is far beyond where it currently is." I sat. Waiting for my guru to reveal the answer to this new train of thought. "You know how you feel when you run well. You know if you are doing what you need to do to be around that PR." He paused and looked at me with a bit more emphasis. "Now. Today. Find something else to push you further, to push yourself beyond what you have done before. You have nothing to lose. As you evaluate your performance in real-time, maybe near the midpoint of the race, find someone in front of you and lock in on them with your eyes. That is your next obstacle to overcome. Don't worry about your PR. Don't worry about finishing the race. You only need to pass your next target."

I nodded my head and paid close attention.

"Each person you pass pulls you along and quickens your pace and gives you a reason to run a bit faster. Once you pass one person, find another, lock in, and continue the cycle. Small goals—small chunks—will help you conquer, not only the race, but your own mind, your own body." He looked down at his watch. "Not sure if you were up for a lecture this morning, but I would be remiss if I let you go today without giving you my pre-race speech."

I nodded, but said nothing at first. "I'm ready. I'm feeling good." I finally replied.

"I'm sure you are. Your coach warned me that the tiger comes out once the gun goes off." He let out a small chuckle. "Well, we should take off in a few minutes to pick up Geno."

* * *

We arrived at the race site at eight forty-five. We checked in and Geno and I spent the next twenty-five minutes warming up. It was getting pretty warm, so we took off our sweats and pinned our race bibs to the front of our jerseys. We did a few final warm-up preparations before heading to the starting line. I was number 109. Geno was number 127. There were just over 200 runners in the race.

As we walked to the starting line, the adrenaline coursed through my body. There were TV cameras and reporters spread throughout, something that was new to me. It was not any bigger than the National Championships I had run in before, but it had a different feeling. The buzz around the race was palpable. There were six of the top US runners in attendance and seven other runners who ranked in the top twenty-five in the world.

I was excited, but nervous. I knew what I wanted to do, but I now had a new focus. I wanted to incorporate Coach Johnson's strategy. It was much like my high school coach's advice about throwing a rope around the runner in front of you and pulling yourself in. I would run my race through 5K and then start locking in on runners in front of me. I was determined to give this a shot.

Geno and I pushed ourselves to a good spot near the front of the group at the starting line. There were still three lines of people in front of us, maybe thirty people or so, but they were all given preferential starting positions. We looked at each other and shook hands.

"See you at the finish," I said.

He nodded his head, "Yup. Push hard and enjoy." A motto that he told me earlier his dad used to say to him.

We stood in our spot for a few minutes. I jumped up and down a few times and took a deep breath. A voice came over the loudspeaker, alerting us to the upcoming start to the race.

Beep... Beep... Bang. The race began and the crowd of runners moved forward with a force I had not experienced before. I was not sure if it was more intense or if I was just in a new aura, maybe something I had manufactured while anticipating the higher level of competition. But soon, maybe twenty-five paces into the race, I was back in my element, running in stride with a group that eventually fell back from the lead pack, but was still moving at a good clip.

At the 2K mark, I was still connected to my original pack of runners. We were within shooting distance of the lead pack, but I could feel them pulling ahead even further. I quickly realized if I didn't pick up the pace soon, they would be out of reach, but I also knew I was well within my PR range, and right now, running a little faster than I anticipated.

Suddenly, a runner broke from my pack and was quickly halfway between my group and the lead. And then, my pack started to trickle apart. Instead of a group, it was a line of runners losing connection. I kept up with two others in my pack as the majority fell behind. I looked forward and the lead pack had also broken apart. The runner who was once with my group had now caught up to and passed a few from the lead group.

My focus started to spread thin. I looked at my group. I look forward at the once tight-knit lead group. I surveyed the long line of runners between me and the lead runners as they rounded a bend up ahead and disappeared. I felt the two runners next to me take off and leave me behind. I was in a situation I was not used to. There were at least two dozen runners distancing themselves from me and now I was being passed by one, two, and then three others.

We hit the 4K mark and two more runners eased their way past. Five K in, I felt I was losing control of the race—I took a deep breath. I began to look inward. I evaluated my pace, my breathing, my strides. I realized I was where I needed to be. I was running my race automatically. I just wasn't used to running my race and still having people cruise past me.

I regained my focus. I glanced at my watch and knew I was on target and let my feet move my body forward. The cadence of my breathing, the swinging of my arms, were where they needed to be.

Once I was back on track I remembered Coach Johnson's words, lock your eyes on one person. And that's what I did. I ran my race, but I added that one new element. I locked in and let that person propel my feet faster. I pulled myself in, just as my high school coach taught me. I combined forces, locking my gaze, throwing my rope, and pulling myself in.

Soon I caught up to two runners, then passed them. I locked in again and did the same. I continued locking in and throwing my rope until I had passed six runners ahead of me. My feet were churning, my eyes were locked in, and I kept pulling myself forward. After a short while, I didn't know how many people I had passed, but I kept on going.

I passed the 7K mark, then the 8. I kept running, I kept speeding up, I kept locking in and throwing my rope. Breathe in... breathe out... lock in, throw the rope... 9K, and soon, the finish in sight.

The big clock above the finish line, large yellow numbers ticking away. I glanced up and my best time was nowhere in sight. It was somewhere in my old self, the old runner that was no longer a part of me. I not only set a new PR, I obliterated it as I breezed past the finish, slowed to a jog, and then a walk. I turned, picked up a cup of water off a table, walked to the side, and waited for Geno to finish.

Chapter Fifteen

Back at home, near the college, I woke up a week later, rested and ready for a three-week break before preseason workouts began. With everything going on the last two years, time had flown by and it was hard to wrap my mind around the fact that I would soon be entering my junior year. But, I put that out of my mind for the time being. My parents were going to visit for a couple days at the end of the week and I was looking forward to seeing them. This would be their first official visit to my college town. I planned on showing them around campus and taking them out to dinner at my favorite restaurant. Other than a few phone calls now and then, and a couple letters here and there, we hadn't talked much outside the three short trips I made home during holidays.

It was a strange feeling. I hadn't had much time to just relax without the singular focus of running and training for the last couple of years. Even during my time with Jade, after our road race, I ran a bit every day. That morning, I lay in bed, thinking about my day. I wasn't quite sure what to do. I did make a pact with myself not to do any running for the next three days. I wanted to give myself a complete physical and mental break, so I would be ready when the season began. I did, though, spend the first hour of the morning writing down my training schedule.

I couldn't help myself.

Mom and Dad showed up on Friday around noon. I took them around campus, showed them the student store and the pub, and then showed them the fieldhouse before meeting my coaches. Their office was located at the top of the fieldhouse building next to the swimming pool and overlooking the track. A slight smell of chlorine filled the stairwell as we climbed the three flights.

After a quick introduction, we sat out on a balcony with a view of the track and the surrounding trees. Off in the distance white clouds and blue skies painted the backdrop above the Evergreens.

We talked for a while, sitting in a circle of comfortable arm-chairs. My mom ended up grilling my coaches a bit, making sure they were looking after her little boy, while my dad asked some questions about the upcoming season and how they thought the team looked. He did throw in a couple questions about me at the end, although he left most of those for my mom. I could tell they were both proud. I was the first of the family to attend college, and not many people from our little town made it this far, especially competing in college sports.

Later that day, after an early dinner at my favorite Italian restaurant, I took them to a park close to my apartment where I enjoyed running. We walked some trails and then sat in the center of the park and reminisced about years past. My mom was a bit nostalgic, looking at her son and seeing the once little boy who would follow her throughout the kitchen, flour caked on hands and face, helping her bake bread and cookies.

"How's Whitie," I inquired.

"Looking kind of old," Dad replied. But, still keeping the young ones in line. And, I think she misses you. She got a bit lethargic after you left. When I go out to feed her she doesn't greet me the way she greeted you."

A lump formed in my throat and I felt a panging for home, which I hadn't really felt since freshman year. "I do miss the animals."

"You're always welcome to come home and spend time with them a bit more often," my mom chimed in with a casual smile. "By the way, Lily was home about a week ago. She wanted me to say hi for her."

"Huh, nice. How's she doing?"

"She said college is going well and that she was going to be transferring to one of the state colleges after she finished up at the junior college. I think she said she would be done by Christmas time. And it sounds like she and her fiance are planning on getting married come spring."

"Nice. Glad to hear." Interestingly, it felt strange hearing Lily's wedding plans. Even with Jade, I still felt a fondness toward Lily and it was hard for me to picture someone else holding her hand, even though I never did.

"She said she would be home for Christmas. If you make it home, maybe you can say hi?"

I hadn't kept my parents up on my relationship with Jade. I wasn't sure what they thought about our relationship, even though they knew I recently visited her for ten days. And Mom talking about Lily led me to believe they didn't know the level of our relationship. I didn't know how to broach it with them, so I just bumbled my way awkwardly. "Well, um, speaking of serious relationships. You know I spent time with Jade, recently."

"Yeah, how'd that go?" my dad asked.

"We had a good time. We trained for the first few days and ran a race together on Saturday, and then we spent time relaxing until I had to leave. There is a nice lake not far from where she lives. It felt like old times back home, running trails and hanging out at the beach. Actually, it was really nice."

"Glad to hear it son," Mom said.

"Right before I left, we started talking." I paused. "We started talking about our future... not just our future together, but what our goals are, what we wanted to achieve with running and with school. We both want the same thing."

"Uh huh..." Mom nodded. Dad looked at me silently, head cocked to the side.

"We both want to be together." I took a breath. "But we also want to finish what we started." Mom smiled. Dad closed his eyes and nodded. "I want to graduate. I want to win a national title... and she has goals of her own to finish up." I took another breath. "But I love her and I really miss her." They sat there, allowing me time to talk, time to express myself. "I finally told her I love her. We both said it for the first time. I think we both already knew it, but we needed to say it." My heart pounded. My voice got softer. It felt good to talk about it, yet I sat there awkwardly. I turned and looked away. "But we both decided that we needed to finish out our final two years of college. And I know that was the right decision, but it's hard."

Mom walked over, sat next to me, and put her arm around my shoulders. We sat there together like we had many times in my young life. I felt I had just skinned my knee and my mom was comforting my childhood sobs. We sat there quietly. I looked off into the distance.

"Son, it's okay for it to be hard. Jade is a lovely girl. If your relationship is meant to be, it will last. You are both doing important things and have made a good decision to stay focused."

I turned and smiled. "I know."

"Remember how quickly your first two years went," Dad added. The next two will be here and gone before you know it. Do what you can to stay focused and your future will come."

"We love Jade," my mom added. "And we want what's best for both of you."

We stood up. I gave a hug to Mom and Dad in turn. We then walked a short lap around the interior of the park, laughing about old times and shaking our heads at how time has rushed by. We then headed back to my place and sat for a little while before my parents hit the road for home.

And now, I was back on my own, two weeks until preseason.

* * *

Half awake the next morning, I lay in bed, mind wandering in and out of dreams—Jade, our time together this summer, running, swimming, relaxing on the beach. I dreamt about our future, wondering what it had in store for us. I saw us walking together in high school, from class to class, hanging out at lunchtime. I pictured us running together after college. It is that connection that makes the distance somewhat bearable. Just knowing that she is running too—just knowing that we have this passion in common—just knowing that running is ours together—helped me tolerate her absence from my life. It also compelled me to continue pushing myself to excel—to run further, harder, more often.

My mom's words rattled around in my head all morning, "... it's Okay for it to be hard. If your relationship is meant to be, it will last." I sat on the edge of my bed, pulled on my training shoes, and laced them up. I hit the pavement and put a few miles between me and my dreams and ran myself a few miles closer to Jade.

As I rounded the corner on the last stretch of my run back to my place, I noticed a few guys hanging around a parked car in front of my building.

"Yo, Running Man." A voice boomed from the group. Running Man is a nickname my teammates started calling me after we saw the movie at the old Cinaplex downtown last year. It's their continual reminder that I do nothing else and I was sure they came to do just that, something other than run.

I smirked and called back, "Wazup, BC?" That was our group's nickname. We would meet for breakfast after our morning workouts during the season last year, so we started calling ourselves The Breakfast Club, or BC for short.

JoJo, a runner built more for combat sports than cross country, turned to the group, "What'd I tell you guys? He was packing in the miles." Everyone let out a moan in unison for emphasis. "We came to take you to the docks one last time. Figured you could use some relaxation before you rev your motor for the season."

"Well, I don't have any plans. Come on up. I'll grab my suit."

JoJo kept me in balance. When he saw me getting myself too deep—training, running, studying, training, running, studying—he would help me pull my head out of my ass and relax. It was nice having a teammate watch out for me. In fact, I credit him with helping me breathe, literally get my breathing back in check. His mantra, "Take a breath, you might live a little longer," was, for me, needed a few times each season.

We spent the next few hours down at the docks, a large lake a few miles from campus with six docks lined with boats outside the Yacht Club. We would spend hours at the end of the docks, diving, swimming, playing grab ass a few times a year. The docks were normally reserved exclusively for paying members, but since we were athletes from the college we were unofficially afforded free entry.

Later, we walked our sun-drenched bodies to our favorite eatery, a small burger joint with the best shakes and greasiest burgers around. It was a treat we rarely indulged in, and only in the off-season. While the burgers were delicious, they sat in your stomach like a lead weight for the rest of the day. It was our final indulgence before preseason in two weeks and we enjoyed every last bite smothered with cheese and topped with fries—our special concoction.

We didn't talk much about running or the season coming up. We knew we would have an overload of that soon. We spent the evening laughing and sharing stories about our summer exploits. It was a much-needed break from life and a bonding time before the season.

Before we headed home for the evening, JoJo broke our unwritten protocol for the night. "I hear we have a couple pretty good freshmen coming in this year." We all turned and looked, expecting him to give us some dirt on the new guys. "That's all I know. Well, that and that the coaches think they both may be good enough to challenge for varsity spots. I guess one of them is a three-time state champ from a big school back east."

"That's good," I answered. "Maybe I'll actually have some help on varsity for once." I gave JoJo a playful shove and then a cold glare. He knew I was halfway joking, but he was also aware of my goals and knew I was reminding him that I expected him to step up this year. He returned my glare and gave me a slight, knowing nod.

* * *

The next two weeks was a fueling-up period. I worked on balancing full-body recovery from a summer of competition with preparing my legs and lungs for the preseason. I was well aware that the first day of preseason would begin with Coach's "reality run." His instructions were simple... "These ten miles will bring reality into focus. Either you are prepared for the season or you are not." I know he didn't expect world-beating times on day one, but he expected a good deal of fitness when we showed up and he made note of who was prepared and who was not.

Week two always began with the "Cardiac Run," which can only be described as a steep climb to a heart attack. It was my job as leader of the varsity to also be the leader on both the reality and cardiac runs and I cherished the thought of being the first to arrive home on both, turning and starting the chant to bring the rest of the team in.

I spent three mornings a week during my fueling-up period in both the weight room and physio. In the mornings I spent long bouts on the treadmill, running hill intervals, and then sets of weighted lunges, squats, and bounding drills. I would then hit an ice bath and sit in the hot tub. On my off days, I ran forty-five to sixty minutes easy, what Coach called, stride runs—runs designed to hit a relaxed pace and work on finding your most comfortable and efficient stride. This type of workout was not to build endurance, but to create a feel for your body, what it could do, and how it performed best. During these workouts, I focused not only on my legs, but also how my arms aided my stride and propelled me forward. I wanted to be able to run without thinking and I ultimately wanted my body to automatically move all parts in their most efficient way from start to finish.

* * *

When my fueling-up period was coming to an end, just two days before preseason, JoJo and I met up at the track. It was a warm morning. The sun was up and beating down on us at eight AM, reminding us that the next couple of weeks would be hot before the cold season slowly rolled in. After a short warm-up run we spent the morning running laps, hills, and buddy carries across the newly lined soccer field inside the track.

The track was empty. We were alone except for the distant sounds of traffic on the busy thoroughfare a few blocks from campus. We finished up our final trudge across the field and back carrying each other one way and then the next and then walked our way slowly around the orange oval that encircled the green grass at its center.

Halfway around, JoJo called my attention to Coach Jay standing by the fieldhouse with five guys we didn't recognize. "I bet those are the freshmen," he said as he squinted through the sun rays toward the distant figures.

"Yup, I'm sure. I remember that nerve-racking walk with Coach a few days before the season. I was scared shitless."

"You and me both." JoJo laughed.

"I remember when you broke loose last year, though," I said to him, throwing my arm around his shoulders and pulling him tight. "When Jimmy got hurt and you were thrown to the wolves, you ran your ass off and got us the win. We had to pick your limp body off the ground and almost give you CPR."

"Holy shit, I've never thrown up that much in my life." He leaned over and reenacted the experience. "I was surprised my shoes didn't end up comin' out of my mouth."

'If a couple of those freshmen can even come close to that,

we'll be pretty good." I added.

"I hope they can. But if they don't, I'm gonna make sure I push you hard enough to win Nationals. I'm gonna be right behind you all season, biting at your heels. Maybe even pass you once in a while." He looked at me with playful determination.

"Okay, don't get ahead of yourself, junior." I let go of his shoulders, turned, and gave him a light shove with both hands on his chest." He stumbled back a couple steps, caught his balance, lowered his head, and charged toward me. His shoulder landed in my belly and we tumbled to the ground. We rolled over and over until we ended up on the green patch of lawn between the track and the fieldhouse. I ended up on top, sat up, and gave him a couple soft pats on the sides of his face. "I told you not to get ahead of yourself, little man. You know I spanked your ass last time we wrestled."

"I ain't through yet, Running Man," He laughed and gave one last effort to get free, popping his hips to the sky, turning, and landing on top of me."

We both collapsed into a pit of laughter when all of a sudden I realized my laughter was turning into a moan, and then I bit my lip in agony. JoJo dismounted, quickly sensing something was wrong.

"What's up? You Okay?" He knelt beside me quickly glancing from my head to my toes.

"I sure fucken hope so," I groaned, lying on my back, eyes closed. I reached with my left hand to my right shoulder. It was throbbing with a dull pain. "Okay, something is definitely wrong with my shoulder."

JoJo looked up to see if Coach was still standing above us, but he wasn't there. "Shit, Coach is gone."

"Good, I hope he didn't see how I got hurt."

"Don't matter, he'll know soon enough."

I sat up and caught my breath. I could feel a cold sweat forming on my forehead and then all of a sudden, I leaned to the side and spewed everything I had left in my stomach.

"Damn, I gotta get you to the trainer. Can you stand?"

I wiped my mouth with the back of my hand and took a deep breath. I stood to my feet. JoJo stood close to steady me. "What time is it?" I asked.

"Eleven."

"Good," I said quietly. "Physio's open until one on Saturdays."

JoJo slowly guided me through the catacomb of hallways in the bottom of the fieldhouse, into the locker room, and to the trainers. He signed me in and a trainer came over to see us.

"What's up, boys," Ron greeted us with his normal energy. "You're holding that shoulder kinda gingerly. What happened?"

I looked at him reluctantly. "We were goofing around and I landed on my shoulder."

Ron directed me to sit on the edge of a padded gray table. "Luckily it's a slow day today."

I smirked and then started to feel the sweat bead up on my forehead again.

"Hold on. Take a deep breath—in—out——in—out." Ron calmed me down and helped me slow my heart rate. I felt the color coming back to my face. He felt around on my shoulder. "Well, you've separated your AC joint. We won't know how severe until you get it x-rayed."

My heart sank.

* * *

154

Later that day, the x-rays confirmed a level three separation of the AC joint in my right shoulder. All the ligaments were torn. Preseason started in two days and I couldn't use my arm. In fact, I was told to keep my arm in a sling and immobile for a minimum of three weeks and then, no sudden movements for two weeks after that. If I wanted full use of my arm while running it would be a full two months at minimum. If I swung my arm with force and my AC joint was not fully healed, recovery would be delayed.

I was devastated and wasn't looking forward to the conversation with Coach Jay. JoJo told me he would come with me to talk to Coach, but I told him I should do it myself. A couple hours later, I was knocking on his door, heart pounding, a lump in my throat. His wife answered and greeted me.

"Coach is in his office. Go ahead and wait in the living room while I get him."

I sat on the couch, feeling sick to my stomach, this time not directly due to the injury, but to the nerves that were coursing through my body. I was dreading the conversation. I felt that I was not only losing my junior year, but letting Coach down, and abandoning my team. I was supposed to be the leader, to carry the team through the season, and here I was, arm strapped to my body, two months away from any reasonable chance to feel the ground below my feet.

"Well, I heard there was an incident at the track after I left," Coach said, shaking his head as he entered the room.

I turned to face him, my heart pounding harder. "Yeah. There was," I replied, clearing my throat.

"I'm glad it happened after your workout. At least the freshmen got to see you hard at work. He paused. "So, what's the prognosis?"

"Popped my AC joint out of place. Tore the tendons. It will be about two months before I can fully run."

"Your legs still work don't they." I couldn't tell if he was serious.

"Yeah. I'm in the best shape of my life."

"I know. I had a good conversation with Coach Johnson about your time in California. He said you are an amazing young man and an even better runner."

"I promise Coach, I'll make up for this."

"I know you will. I've watched you for the past two years grow from a scrawny freshman barely able to keep your feet under you to leading the team, and with a shot to break the remaining school records you haven't broken already."

"I promise. I will. I'll be back stronger than I am now."

"Of course and I'm going to hold you to it."

"I want you to and I'm going to be in the weight room and the training room every day, twice a day."

"And you'll be at practice every day, too. You think you worked hard before... You'll need every ounce of strength to recover and continue leading the team. The guys need you there and you need to be there to stay connected."

"For sure, Coach. I've mapped it out. I should be back in eight weeks, October 21. That gives me time to be ready for Regionals. I'll be there every step of the way with the team, and I'll make sure I'm ready."

"I know you will. Make sure to get to physio on Monday before practice, set up your rehab schedule, and then meet with the team on the track. There'll be a stationary bike and a workout waiting for you." My heart rate slowed. My nerves subsided. "If you want to make this work, you can. But it's gonna take extreme focus." He smiled.

We sat and talked for a while longer. He asked me about my

experiences in California and about my training. We talked about my classes and what it will take to stay on track with my studies and the added recovery work. He was supportive, but he also made it clear that it wasn't going to be easy. "Adversity is what makes true champions," was the last thing he said as I left for the night.

Chapter Sixteen

Day one of preseason was harder than I thought. I made my physio appointments for the next eight weeks and met the team on the track. Coach introduced the new freshmen and a new transfer, a junior who was supposed to fill the hole our graduating seniors left last season. I gave them a rousing speech about working hard and dedicating to academics and running and then Coach sent them on their day-one workout. My heart sank as I watched them trail off into the distance.

"Whatcha waiting for captain," Coach barked. "You have a workout in front of you." And there it was, the dreaded stationary bike and a journal sitting on the seat. I opened it up to the first page, jumped on the bike, and read my instructions. "After each workout, log your information, and return it to the box outside my office. I'll return it to you each day at practice with instructions." I nodded and began peddling away.

The next few weeks were the same. And I still couldn't get the pit in my stomach to go away every time I watched my teammates take off for the day's run. There was one bright spot, though. We started two a day workouts week two and we met in the weight room every morning at six thirty. I enjoyed that time the most, as I was able to stay with the team and do some of the work out with them.

I went to physical therapy three times a week for the first two weeks and then five times a week for the next two weeks. Ron, the trainer, was there every day, monitoring my progress. At the end of week four he said I was right on track. I had been working out strictly on the stationary bike for cardio to make sure I didn't jostle my shoulder and disrupt the healing, but now he told me to work three days a week on the stairmaster for the next two weeks.

I was pushing myself hard, at least as hard as I could on the cardio equipment, but it just wasn't the same. I could tell that my lungs were not as strong as they were in August. And even though I had been working my legs in the weight room, I was missing the road mileage.

Week five I added two days a week on the treadmill and upped it to three days in week six. The only problem was, I had to strap my arm to my body and had to keep my pace slow. It felt like I was almost walking. I could feel my body depleting. No matter how hard I wanted to work, I could only push my injury so hard.

Week seven rolled around and I was able to unstrap my arm and run at a quicker pace without swinging my arm. It felt nice, but I was chomping at the bit to let my body fly. Each day at practice I watched my teammates take off, stronger each time, and return, drenched in sweat one day, rain and mud the next. I was starting to feel disconnected. I was starting to see my season slip away.

Week eight was finally here. It was time to start testing my arm. Ron told me my AC joint was strong, but he wanted to make sure I didn't break up the scar tissue, otherwise it would be painful and hinder the movement of my arm. By the end of the week he was convinced I was ready to run. Friday I ran a mile around the track. He checked my shoulder and it was good. On

Saturday I ran three miles. He checked it again and signed off on my medical release.

I was ecstatic. I could hardly contain my excitement, yet I was nervous, not that I would re-injure myself, but how I would feel running with the team. I knew they were in top shape. They had already competed in five meets. JoJo led the pack and actually won a race for the first time. The new transfer was good too, pushing JoJo to the limit, taking second to JoJo once and coming in just behind him in the other meets. Two freshmen had made a big impact in meets, as well. The team had gelled without me and fared well in the conference. I felt like a freshman all over again, trying to find my place on the team.

* * *

Monday came around. I was happy it was a light day, the team recovering from a difficult meet on Saturday. We took to the track for a half-mile warm-up. I ran alongside JoJo and the New Guy. I felt good—back on the track with the team. We then took off into the trails for a three-mile jog. I quickly felt the difference. Normally, I would jump out front, set the pace, and lead. Suddenly, it was JoJo out front. Without a word, he set the pace and I followed two behind, the New Guy was right on JoJos heels. I had to force myself not to compete, not to try and overtake them, but at the same time the urge to run was coursing through my body.

When we were done, I was surprised how much JoJo had improved over the last eight weeks and just how much conditioning I had lost. A few weeks ago three miles would have been a breeze and JoJo would have been in my rearview mirror. Today, while I finished the three miles relatively easily, I had to work to keep up to someone who usually struggled to keep up with me.

I had a competition this weekend and two weeks until Region-als. There was a lot of ground to make up. This was the first time since I moved to varsity almost two years ago that a seed of doubt crept into my mind. *Did I have it in me? Was there enough time to prepare?*

That night, as I lay in bed, those two questions filtered through my dreams. And, when I woke up, they were foremost on my mind.

* * *

Tuesday: Four miles. We finished with a set of hills. With each hill I was invigorated, but also questioned my body. If this was early September I would be okay. I would have the time to make up my deficit. But, I was still behind and I wasn't sure I could make up for lost time.

Wednesday: Intervals around a set of baseball and softball fields. I kept up just fine on lap one. Two-minute rest. I managed to lead the pack by a couple of strides on lap two. Two minute rest. I just edged JoJo on lap three. Lap four, I struggled to stay stride for stride. My lungs began to show their preseason form. Lap five, I Finished behind JoJo and the New Guy. And lap six. Finished. Hands on knees, behind a freshman. And, the question emerged again, *Do I have it in me?*

Thursday: We tapered for Saturday's final meet of the season. Fortunately for me, a simple run, warm down, and stretching.

The best part of practice came in my fourth physio check-up of the week. "Your AC joint is holding strong," Ron told me. "Keep coming after each workout, but it appears your body is cooperating." A feeling of relief overtook me for a brief moment, but then I thought, *Now, only if my legs and lungs agreed with you.*

* * *

Friday: We took off early for a six-hour drive. I was anxious. My first active competition of the season was the next day. Last year, I blasted the course record by eleven seconds, but that was far from my thoughts. I knew the course well and as I lay my head on the back of the bench seat in the rear of the team van, I ran my normal strategy through my mind, realizing it would not work this time. Normally, I started off strong and picked up the pace. The last two times I ran this course I was in the lead by the quarter-mile mark and finished well ahead of second place.

This time I decided to hold back my urge to start fast. I knew if I went out too strong I would blow my wad halfway out. I decided to stay just off JoJo's pace. I figured if nothing else, he would be close enough to the leaders that I could make a push at the end.

JoJo ran a strong race from start to finish and went out faster than I had anticipated. I had nothing in the tank for the final stretch. I placed fifth behind two guys from a rival college and JoJo and the New Guy took third and fourth. I finished two minutes and twenty-seven seconds off my record-setting time. The winner was just nine seconds off my record.

Do I have it in me? This time the question boomed, rattled, and bounced around inside my head. Nine days until Regionals.

* * *

I woke up Sunday morning in my bed. I felt a slight pain in my shoulder. As I got up I realized I had slept all night on my right side, something I had made a concerted effort not to do during

162

my recovery. I got out of bed, popped a couple aspirin, ate a banana, and slid on my runners. I walked outside. A slight mist fell from the low-hanging fog.

I was out on the road on my own, something I loved, but hadn't done since the summer. It felt freeing. I took a deep breath and felt my running partner beside me. Jade's presence was comforting, like always. I pictured our runs around the lake this past summer. My heart warmed.

I finished the run with a solid half-mile push and then slowly jogged once around my apartment building, picturing myself at my peak and remembering how I felt in California, passing runner after runner.

I came to a stop at my front door, but did not go in. I stood, breathing quietly, hands on hips, eyes closed. *Do I have it in me?* The question sat in my mind. I let air fill my lungs, held it for a moment, and then let it out slowly... "I do," I said out loud. Maybe not in my legs. Maybe not in my lungs. But I have it in my mind. *I can will myself to run. I know my body. I can will it to do what it is trained to do.*

* * *

Nine days later, I was shoulder to shoulder with 250 other runners on a wide-open field—blood coursing through my body. A mad dash as the race commenced. JoJo on my left, the New Guy on my right. I pushed to find the lead, but was quickly boxed in as the open field funneled into a compact three-runner-wide trail. I kept pace, just behind the lead pack, looking for an opening. I gazed forward and saw the trail opening up just ahead. I pushed to keep pace. I struggled to stay balanced as bodies pushed to move forward.

The trail opened up. I bounded forward and locked my eyes on the lead pack of four. I zoned in. I threw my rope around the runner at the back of the pack. I moved my feet—steadied my breathing. I swung my arms. If my right shoulder could scream it would have cried out in pain. I ran hard. I drove my legs. I pulled myself in. I caught up with the lead pack just as the front runner took off.

A half mile left. I caught the lead runner with my gaze and began pulling myself forward. A quarter mile to go. The finish in sight. I pushed harder. My lungs burned. My legs heavy. I willed myself forward.

Finally, shoulder to shoulder, I caught up and was now stride for stride with the front runner. My eyes were fixed on the finish line. I pushed—I bound—I leapt—crossing the line a fraction ahead. I collapsed to the ground in both relief and exhaustion. But now, as I lay supine on the ground, my body began to seize. My right leg cramped and my breathing became erratic. I had pushed my body past its limits. That's what my mind was trained to do. This time, though, I had gone too far. Just over two months ago, I was in the best shape of my life and was coming off the best race of my career. Now, with the injury and the time off, my body was not prepared and was paying the price.

I felt two sets of hands cradle my body and help me to my feet and off to the side. I was placed on a cot and given fluids. I felt nauseous. I didn't want to open my eyes.

I heard Coach Jay's familiar voice, "How you feeling?"

I slowly opened my eyes. "A little better now." I paused and then asked, "How'd I do?"

"Other than running a miraculous race and winning by less than a second, you almost killed yourself. Well, not literally, but you tried."

"I'm not sure what I was doing. My body just took over."

"It sure did. Now, let's work on helping your body recover."

* * *

When I woke up the next morning, I felt a tightness and a dull throbbing in the back of my right leg. I got up and a stiffness ran from the back of my right knee up through my buttocks. I limped over to my desk and took a couple aspirin and then found enough ice in the freezer to keep the back of my leg frozen intermittently throughout the day.

After lunch, I went for a slow walk outside. Normally I would go for a short recovery run, but my body was in no condition to walk fast, let alone run.

The next day I went to the trainer first thing in the morning. I found out I had a strained hamstring and was advised to stay off it for an entire week. Luckily, Nationals wasn't for two weeks, but unfortunately, I couldn't train. I would have to find a way to maintain what little endurance I had left in my body. By Wednesday the trainer reluctantly allowed me on the stationary bike. I'm sure it was to appease me, knowing that I was ready to burst and go for an all-out, balls-to-the-wall run, body ready or not. By Sunday I could jog up to two miles on the track. I was able to run a relaxed 5K by the Wednesday before Nationals. On Friday I felt good enough to jog the course a day before the race.

The day of the Championships, I was as ready as I could be. I had warmed up with the team and was standing on the starting line with runners from across the country waiting for the race to begin. This is not how I wanted it to be. I knew I was not at my normal level, mentally or physically. I tried my best to psych myself up, to block out the question that had again floated into my head, *Do I have it in me?* But this time I answered... not today. I could feel a fist-size tightness in the back of my leg, and instinctively knew if I pushed too hard I could end up with a complete tear.

In order to get through the race I would have to take it slow for at least half the race to make sure my body was entirely warm and my hamstring was as loose as it could get. And, that is what I did. Just about halfway through the race, I could feel the fist in my hamstring relax enough for me to run at a decent pace, but I still had to shorten my stride. I ended up finishing a few places behind JoJo and the New Guy and about fifty places behind where I finished my sophomore year, not even All-American honors within sight.

With everything I went through the last three months, I knew I should be proud of how I finished, but I couldn't allow myself to be. Instead, I was frustrated. I couldn't stop thinking about all the training I put in the last two years. I was poised to be the best in the Nation. If I had only run even close to how I had run in California I would have won standing up. But, that's not what happened—and I couldn't let it go.

Chapter Seventeen

January rolled around and I was out of shape for the first time since I was in middle school. I took a full two months off to let my hamstring heal. I spent four days a week in the training room getting it worked on, but I just couldn't find my way to do any training, even though after three weeks I was cleared to ride the stationary bike and do some lifting.

I spent my entire winter break back home with my parents. I even rode the boat into town with my dad twice when the weather broke just enough. I helped Mom in the kitchen a bit and did some of my old chores. It felt nice, but it also allowed me to hide away. I pulled back and used my time at our house by the lake to wallow in pity. I didn't let anybody know, but when the lights went out at night and all was quiet, I drowned in my sorrow.

It was refreshing walking the winter trails around my childhood home. I visited Lily and met her fiance. I had dinner with Jade's parents twice and shared stories about my time with Jade this past summer. Jade was not able to come home. She was involved in an internship that carried through the break. But, I enjoyed my time with her family.

By the time I was back in my college home, I felt a distance from running. Part of it was my frustration turned to self-pity.

Part of it was that it was the off-season and my normal self-motivation was replaced by recovery. I had convinced myself that a total break was good for my mind and body and to an extent that was true, but I took it to an extreme. I should have jumped right back into therapy when I returned. I should have jumped on the stationary bike and the stair climber, and started some easy runs on the track. But, classes started the third week of January, and then February hit and I had done nothing, but go to class, study, and call Jade twice a week.

One night in early February I lay in bed, feeling a bit more sheepish than normal. Coach Jay called me earlier in the day and asked me to stop by his office to talk about my recovery and training. Since I had been back I shied away from the fieldhouse, the track, my teammates, and my coaches. I didn't know how to approach anything connected to running at this point and I was sure that's why Coach contacted me.

I woke up the next morning feeling sick. It was even worse than the feeling I had when I first told Coach about my injury. I felt physically nauseous. I ran to my bathroom and retched into the toilet. I squatted down and let my forehead rest on the cold porcelain bowl. I wasn't sure why I was allowing myself to feel this way, why I let everything I had worked for over the past three seasons slip away.

* * *

I walked into Coach's office at nine AM. He was on an animated phone call. He was waving his hands and laughing into the receiver as if he was watching a stand-up comedian.

At least he's in a good mood, I thought. He hung up the phone and looked at me with a big smile.

"Sorry about that." I was talking to Coach Johnson. We haven't talked since last summer. He told me you and one of his runners connected while you were there. I think his name was Geno.

"Yeah, Geno. He's cool."

"I guess Geno told him you guys talked about meeting up next summer after your senior year was over."

"Oh, yeah. He invited me to go on some hiking trips."

"Sounds like a nice guy." He paused. "Anyway, I just wanted to check in with you since I haven't seen you around for a while."

"I've been focusing on my classes. I have a lot of work in Anatomy and Kinesiology."

"I get it." He nodded. "I also wanted to check in on how you are feeling physically. Ron told me you haven't been to therapy since the new semester started."

"I know."

"Can you fit in a couple mornings a week?"

"Maybe." I took a deep breath. My eyes started to dampen. My breathing became shallow. I felt a lone tear slowly make its way down my cheek.

We sat in silence for a minute.

"JoJo said you've been keeping your distance from the guys. Said he has asked you to meet him at the pub a few times and you didn't show."

I sat in shame—in fear, not sure what I was ashamed or scared of. Tears streamed down my face.

Coach stood up, walked from behind his desk, and sat next to me. He sat on the edge of his chair and leaned forward with his hands on his knees. "Running is just a small part of life. I know when you're in the middle of it, it feels like everything. But there is much more to life than winning a race." He softly placed his hand on my shoulder. "I know the amount of time and effort you've put into your training. And I know you had a shot at Nationals if all went right. But, it didn't, and you still put everything on the line." We sat in silence. My tears slowed.

"There is also more to running than coming in first." He continued. "Running is about the ups and downs, about the obstacles, about overcoming the things that get in your way." He paused, stood up, and looked out the window toward the track below. "Running is about finding yourself. It is about who you become after putting in all the miles. The miles late at night. The miles early in the morning. The miles in the scorching sun or the wind and rain." He turned back to me. "The question now, for you, is how do you want to face your obstacles? What do you want to have learned about yourself after all the miles."

He stopped and sat on the edge of his desk facing me. "Enough of my lecture. I want you to meet me on the track tomorrow morning at seven. Just you and me. Bring your running shoes. I know it's Saturday, but from what I can tell, you haven't been doing much on the weekends. And don't worry. Just be ready for some good old-fashioned fun."

* * *

I met Coach Jay the next morning. We strapped on our shoes and took a nice easy jog off campus to his "favorite coffee shop." We sipped on our drinks for an hour or so. He shared stories about some of the better runners he had coached. He told me about a young guy about a dozen years earlier who was just under three seconds out of Olympic qualifying pace in the 10,000 meters. He told me how it was difficult for him to recover mentally from the disappointment of missing out on his lifelong dream. But now he is a successful coach himself and still competes occasionally.

I told him about Jade, how I got into running, and how running makes me feel connected to her when we are apart. It felt strange sharing that with him for some reason, but it was also a relief.

We jogged the two miles back to campus in silence. I'm sure the silence was purposeful on his part, giving me time to think and soak in our conversation. But for me, it was out of necessity. I didn't know what to say or really how to feel. I let my body relax as my feet hit the pavement and moved me forward.

Even though running had been most of my life since ninth grade, it felt foreign to me at this point, as if I was an infant learning to walk.

Chapter Eighteen

The following Monday, I did visit Ron in the training room. He set me up with some simple stretching and strengthening exercises twice a week. At the end of the week, I went on my first solo run in months, not because I really wanted to, but because I felt an obligation to Coach Jay. He never told me I had to start running again, but I felt if I put in a few miles each week I would be doing right by him.

By mid-March, I was back to a cursory schedule of physio and training. I wasn't doing anything hard, but I was running three to six miles three to four days a week. I met JoJo for lunch on Wednesdays and we ran together once or twice a week. I was working my way back into my regular life. I didn't feel like a hermit anymore, but I was far from motivated to do anything strenuous.

April came around and I was doing much of the same, kind of going through the motions—physio and a few miles a week. Spring break was just around the corner and I was glad. I needed a break from my classes. Along with Anatomy and Kinesiology, I was struggling through upper-level physics and biology classes.

The Friday before Spring break I was warming up on the track. I rounded the final corner on my first of two laps and looked toward the fieldhouse and saw my assistant coach standing next to Old Man #2. I stuck my hand in the air and waved. They both nodded.

As I finished my second lap, they were gone and I took off for a run around the campus trails. When I arrived back, my assistant coach was standing near the track by himself. He waved me over.

"How's it going?" he called out to me as I neared him.

"Run felt good."

"Nice. But, how are you doing?"

I guess I should be glad people were checking in on me, but for some reason, I wasn't. "Uh, better. I seem to be getting my feet under me."

"What are you doing during break?" He asked with a serious look on his face.

"Same thing I'm doing now."

"So, you'll be around?"

"Yeah. I'll be up here on Tuesday and Thursday morning for physio."

"Great, would you mind if an old man joined you for a run sometime next week?"

"Sure, I could use the company." I was assuming he was going to be doing much of what Coach Jay did when we jogged to the coffee shop.

"Are you free Friday morning? I can meet you at your apartment around seven."

"That works."

"I'll introduce you to a new course that's kinda fun."

"Okay."

"Well, I've got a phone call to make. See you next week?"

"Yup, see yuh then." I watched him walk away. I was a bit confused. He had never reached out to me like this outside the confines of the team. But, I ended up brushing it off and putting it out of my mind.

* * *

Friday morning was upon me. I wasn't sure what to expect, so I got up early enough to have my normal oatmeal pre-run breakfast and then I waited outside for Coach to arrive. He drove up in his Mustang. The guys on the team razzed him about his midnight blue, convertible, mid-life-crisis mobile, but really, we were all a bit jealous. It was a beautiful machine.

I hopped in, and he told me that I would have to squeeze in the back in a few minutes because we were picking up one more person. I turned around and checked out the back seat, "I'm sure I can fit back there," I replied with a quiet laugh.

We drove down a winding road through a couple of neighborhoods I had never seen before. "Here we are," Coach announced. We were stopped in front of an old brown, mid-century-style home with large evergreens along each side. "You mind running up and letting him know we are here."

I looked at him confused. "Who are we picking up?"

"A friend of mine. Don't worry. He knows you're coming."

I got out of the car, feeling a little wary. *What was Coach hiding?* I thought.

I rang the doorbell and waited until a familiar face appeared on the other side of the door. Old Man #2 was standing there, dressed in his running gear, with a big smile on his face. "How's it going, young man? You lookin' forward to a nice run this morning?"

I nodded, and not knowing what else to say, replied, "Wow, you got a nice house."

"Thanks. It does the job." He walked through the open door and closed it behind him. "Well, let's head out. I've been looking forward to running with you again. It's been a couple of years." I knew he was referring to my freshman year. The mock race Coach set up with his running buddies.

"Yeah, not since my freshman year."

I jumped in the back seat and settled myself between two duffle bags. Old Man #2 got in and closed the door. He turned around, looked at me, and smiled, then turned to Coach. "You ready this morning, Coach."

"Sure am. It should be fun."

I could tell something was up. Their cryptic messages read loud and clear, but still didn't give away their hidden secret.

As we drove down the road, Old Man #2 asked me how school was going and then slipped in a couple questions about my training. "I've seen you running a few times around campus this spring." He finally said. "Actually, Coach asked me to come watch."

"What do you mean, come watch?" I asked.

"To tell you the truth, ever since we ran together your freshman year, I've followed your career. Your performance down at the California invite was amazing. I wish I had been there to witness it. First in your age group and twelfth overall. You must have been ecstatic."

"Yeah. It was a blast."

"So, I have seen you run a bit over the last few months and I've been concerned."

"About what?" Even though I knew what he was referring to and had the same concern, I kept that to myself.

"You had a rough go of it this past season and it doesn't seem like you've let it go."

"Let go of what?"

"Your disappointment."

"I'm just giving myself some space to recover."

"It looks to me like more than that." We sat quietly for a few minutes before he broke the silence. "Sometimes disappointment can turn into more if you don't deal with it." I had no reply. "And it seems to me it has rooted deeper." I closed my eyes. "Maybe depression. Maybe self-doubt," he concluded.

We rounded the corner. I looked out the window and there was a group of about a dozen men standing together by a blue pop-up awning. *I knew they were hiding something,* I told myself.

We pulled into a dirt lot and parked next to a few other cars. "Here we are," Coach said matter-of-factly as he turned off the car. We got out and walked over to the group of runners. Under the tent was a padded massage bench, a few coolers full of ice and bottled water, and a table full of protein bars and oranges.

Coach introduced me to the gaggle of runners and then urged me to down a protein bar and water. As I sat on a chair and followed my instructions, a few of the gaggle came up to me and asked how I was feeling.

"I guess okay. Although, I'm not sure what's going on."

"This is our running group," one of the gaggle told me. "I heard you were recruited to join us on our annual run."

"Yeah, seems like it." I stood up and downed the last swig of water. "What are we running?

"The same run we do every spring."

"We call it the sewage run," another of the gaggle added.

I knew there was a sewage plant nearby with an open culvert that ran parallel to the road for a few miles. That didn't sound too inviting, though. "So you run along the sewage line... whoever came up with that?" I ask, a little annoyed.

"One of our former members, about ten years ago. And it ain't just along the sewage ditch." The first member of the gaggle said. "Why don't we let your coach fill you in. Hey Coach, your boy here wants to know what he got himself into. You wanna fill him in?"

Coach came over and put his arm around me, "I guess he deserves to know." He smiled, stepped back and looked at me. "About ten years ago, the club founder came up with the idea to have an annual run to celebrate our time on the road. It started out as the sewage run because his famous saying was, "If you love to run, you will run anywhere." So we started out running from the sewage plant along the sewage line and to the park in the center of town. It was about seven miles. Over the next few years, it was revamped two or three times—first time to half marathon and the final time to a full marathon, but always running by the sewage ditch."

I took a deep breath and tried to hide my shock.

"So what do yuh think?" A voice came from behind me. I turned to see, Old Man #1, the one runner that beat me in the race my freshman year, leaning against the massage table with a water in his hand.

"Ummm, I'm not sure what to think. I've never thought about running a marathon. I've never even run more than thirteen miles at one time." I stopped talking and stood still. And finally, I said to myself, "and I'm not prepared for this."

Coach came up to me again. "You are more than capable... we're not looking for record-setting times. In fact, we are not looking for times at all. We purposefully don't keep official time. If people want to keep time on their own, that's fine, but we are here just to run and enjoy what we love most—to run and to run with our friends who also love to run."

"You are a beautiful runner. You've proved that time and time again," Old Man #2 chimed in. "I experienced it firsthand the one time we ran together. You need to put the obstacles of the last season behind you and find yourself again. We brought you here today to help you find the joy of running again, without any expectations."

"Okay, gentleman," a voice came from outside the tent. "Let's get ready."

We walked out as a group. I looked around, bewildered, stunned, that I was standing a short time from just over twenty-six miles. I took my sweats off, hung them on a hook by the tent, bent over, tightened my laces, and stood there, hands on my hips. I looked around, everyone else was hopping up and down or stretching or taking off for a short jog. I was a statue. I was frozen. At least on the outside. Internally, I was shaking. My blood was pounding, rushing through my veins, not to warm up my body, but rather, to find a place to hide.

"Hey, Running Man," Coach called out. "Come on, startling me out of my daze. Let's get that body warmed up." He never called me that before. But, I heeded his call and ran to catch up.

As I slowly jogged around and tried to catch my bearings, I realized nobody had asked if I wanted to join in. Nobody had asked if I wanted to put my body through the hell it was soon to endure. I don't think they assumed. I don't think they thought. I think they just acted. I think they just decided this is what I needed to do. I felt like turning and running the other way— turning and running away— turning and finding anywhere else to be other than where I was currently at. I was not only nervous, I was scared. The haunting question filtered through my mind once again, *Do I have it in me?* But I was too scared to answer this time.

The last five months I had allowed myself to drift away from what had been my life. I allowed myself to cower, and that is what I was now used to doing. But this time I was surrounded—I was surrounded by others who loved running as much as I had up until just a few months ago. I felt trapped, so I stayed, against what I thought was my better judgment.

Soon we were all at the starting line, an intimate group of runners, just fifteen of us, ready to break free and run. I stood there, heart pounding, stomach churning, body shaking—Coach on my left—Old Man #2 on my right.

A whistle blew and we were off. I didn't know what to expect—how hard to go out. I just followed. It started off as a casual run and I kept stride with the men beside me.

Soon, we were two miles in and I was feeling pretty good. I also knew there was a long way to go, so I kept up the easy pace. Not long after, we had completed 5K, and then 10K... and we kept on going.

After we reached the halfway mark, I realized I was doing okay. We had run at such a leisurely pace that my body was doing just fine. I was so used to pushing hard and running to win that it felt freeing to just run.

I found myself lost in thought a mile or two later and then realized I was alone between two small groups of runners. I took a quick peek over my shoulder and saw, quite a ways back, coach and Old Man #2, and a few others keeping pace with each other. In front of me were a few runners I didn't know.

As I continued to run, my thoughts began to wander. I thought about Jade. I thought about the race in California. I thought about the end to my junior season, the qualifying race for Nationals, where I ran myself into the ground, and my disappointing finish at Nationals.

All of a sudden, I realized I was just a few paces behind the group in front of me. I wasn't sure how I caught up. My body was running on autopilot and doing what it had been trained to do over years of running—push and run faster. So, that's what it did.

I ended up passing the three runners who were in front of me and I continued moving forward. I was amazed by the swiftness of my gait as my feet moved my body along the path.

But, not long after, with just a few miles to go, I could feel my body losing steam. I grabbed water from a table that was placed at the side of the course, drank it down, and tossed it to the side.

My feet kept moving. My legs kept churning. But, quickly, I was zapped of energy, and my head began to spin.

Rounding the bend, the sun struggled to find its way through gray skies. Tamped gravel led the way down the path. Trees on the left created a canopy, blocking the view of the sewage culvert that flowed along the final six miles of the course. My feet moved forward slowly. I struggled to find air. Erratic breaths, wheezed in—and then out—and then in again, between parched lips. I blinked. I ran slowly. One foot, the next foot, each connected to tree trunks that once were legs. Heavy and awkward, I labored to keep my balance on the trunks that held me up and moved me forward. One foot forward. The next dragged and followed. I wobbled to one side, fought to regain balance—one stride, two strides, stumble, balance, step forward, stride, stumble, stride. My body was trained to continue moving, but had lost equilibrium and began weaving left, right, left... step forward, then back, left, then right, stumble forward.

Hands from behind grasped under my armpits and held me steady, yet continued to move me forward. A low gravely whisper, "Move forward. One foot. The next foot. Move forward." For some reason, my body listened. "One foot. The next foot. Move forward," the whisper came again.

I continued. Wheezing in. Wheezing out. Moving forward. Tree Trunks—balance—whisper repeated.

The whisper comforted, "Move forward. One foot. The next foot," as a cup of water was emptied over my head.

Water wetted my hair and dripped down my face.

Hands released my body.

I struggled to continue moving. Whisper repeated... "Move forward."

Hand gripped my wrist and urged me to continue. "Move forward. One foot. The next foot. Move forward."

Hand pulled me forward silently.

I began to move—to move more—to again move with a sense of purpose. Trunks began to lighten. Legs returned. Breathing slowed and regulated. I continued to follow the hand on my wrist. I gained strength with each step, enough to run as if my body knew where it was going.

Hand let go. Feet continued to move. Breathe in—Breathe out. Lungs filled and fueled my body. Feet moved forward.

The hand that held my wrist now ran beside me in tandem. It was Old Man #2. We ran together, quietly, but at a good pace and with life. Trees wished by on the left. Gravel crunched underfoot.

I managed my breathing and controlled my gait. My legs moved forward on their own, in stride, as they were trained to do. On cue, my arms began to churn with force, swishing, one and then the other, on opposite sides of my body.

I lifted my eyes and peered forward. Some ways off in the distance, I saw the end. The finish was near, within my grasp.

I picked up my pace. My strides lengthened. My breathing deepened and slowed. I begin to run without effort—my feet bounding, gliding, not touching the ground. I floated, I flew, I ran on clouds above the gravel pathway.

Striding forward, I felt nothing, save the wind through my body. All weight, all effort transformed into energy propelling me forward, faster and faster, to the end.

Trees ripped by on the left. Old Man #2 glided next to me, stride for stride. But I heard nothing.

Running continued. Feet moved forward, afloat, not touching the ground.

Without effort, I pulled myself in. My arms pumped. My legs floated, one in front of the other.

I was out of body, yet fully within and connected, totally cognizant of my weightlessness.

I ran free.

I came to the end.

I slowed down.

I walked.

I dropped to my knees.

Old Man #2 joined me on the ground. He rolled over on his back and let out a loud yelp and then began to laugh. "You did it," he said. "You did it."

I lay quietly, in a half daze.

Time passed, I remained on the ground, regaining my senses. Someone came over and poured water on my face and body and handed me a bottled water. Soon, I heard a few more footsteps as others crossed the finish. I sat up and took a swig of the cold liquid. I looked up just in time to see Coach cross the line with another runner. They slowed down, turned, and slapped hands.

I looked around. A few of the runners were walking around, cooling their bodies. A few sat on the ground exhausted. One man was being attended to on the training table in the tent.

I heard two men talking behind me. It sounded like a couple runners didn't finish the race, but were okay.

I was still a bit groggy, but made my way to my feet. Coach was walking around and stretching his body. He came over and stood in front of me. He put his hands, one on each of my shoulders, as I worked to gain my balance. He helped me walk over to a cooler of water and told me to drink.

I gulped down three cups of water through parched lips. My head felt light, but over the next few minutes, I regained my mind and body. I sat on a chair by the tent and ate a protein bar. My stomach felt hollow and the morsels of food felt like they hit an empty pit as I swallowed.

I sat still, taking deep, deliberate breaths, helping to circulate the oxygen around my body. I heard quiet conversations around me. Runners were all taking their time, allowing their bodies to recover, enough at least so they could breathe with regularity.

Old Man #2 walked slowly toward me. He looked a bit pekid, but he managed to shoot me a smile. "So, now what do you think of this yearly tradition?" He chirped with as much enthusiasm as he could muster.

I swallowed down what was in my mouth and cleared my throat. "I'm still in a bit of a daze. Not sure I can make an accurate assessment at this point," I chuckled. "You guys are crazy." I shook my head.

"You're one of us now—one of the crazy ones." He stuck out his hand. I reached out and grabbed it and he pulled me up to my feet. We walked around and stretched, saying little, except for a few grunts and groans as we tried to get our bodies to cooperate.

After a labored warm-down and stretch, we met Coach by the tent. He was talking to a few of the other runners. He introduced me to them and gave me a little background. Most of them were pretty accomplished runners. A couple had competed nationally and internationally with success and those are the ones that finished in front of me. A couple others ran in college and joined the club to keep a connection with the sport. I knew a little about my coach already. He was a 2x DII All-American in the 5,000 and 10,000 meters and ran for USA track for a number of years after he graduated. But I knew little to nothing about Old Man #2, other than he lived in a cool Mid-Century home ten minutes from campus.

So, I turned to Old Man#2. "What about you?"

"What about me?" He grinned.

"What's your stake in all this? Why are you here?"

"It's not an interesting story."

"Okay. But, you got me into this, so tell me anyway."

"I ran in college and got hurt. Once I recovered I was never the same. And then, later in life I started running again and found the enjoyment that I had lost."

"Don't be modest," Coach interrupted. "He was one of the top recruits coming out of high school and participated in the Olympic trials the spring before his freshman year."

"So, you were pretty good?" I asked.

"I was decent. But I never got to follow through. I never got to finish what I started."

I looked at him and smiled. "Hmmmph," I replied and nodded knowingly.

Chapter Nineteen

I woke up the next morning. My body felt heavy. I lay in bed contemplating breakfast as my stomach felt emptier than usual, but nothing sounded good. I lay there going in and out of sleep for another hour and finally forced myself to sit up. I walked to the kitchen, grabbed a glass from the cupboard, and filled it with tap water. My mouth was dry. I drank it down. I stood for a moment and drank another. I leaned over the sink, hands poised on the edge, balancing my depleted body.

I turned and walked over to the fridge and opened the door. I stared into the abyss. I knew I should eat something, but nothing looked appetizing. I reached in and shuffled through a few small containers of leftovers. I pushed them aside. I pulled out the one thing I thought my body could handle, a single serving vanilla yogurt.

I sat at the counter slowly spooning the white substance into my mouth. I could feel it coating my stomach and the pang of emptiness began to dissolve. After I finished, I walked over to the couch, plopped down, and pulled the blanket over my body. When I opened my eyes, it was two hours later.

I pushed myself up and sat on the edge of the couch. It was eleven o'clock. I felt a bit better, so I got up, ate a piece of cheese and a hard-boiled egg left over from breakfast earlier in the week.

I changed into sweats and sneakers and decided to go to physio for an ice bath and a soak in the hot tub. If I hurried I would have just enough time. Since it was Saturday, it closed at one, but I knew the effort would be worth it.

And it was. I felt a lot better after I dried my body and dressed. I walked to the pub on campus and bought a ham and cheese sandwich. Halfway through my meal, my body started to respond to the nutrients. I could feel the blood running through my body and coloring my face. While I wasn't fully recovered, which would take almost a week, I was feeling human again.

I sat, nibbling on the second half of my sandwich when I heard my name from across the room. It was Joseph, the guy I tried to stand up for a couple years back. I hadn't seen him in a long time. I stood up and walked toward him. He met me halfway.

We shook hands and exchanged greetings.

"What you been up to lately?" Joseph asked. "Haven't seen you around for a while."

"Running and studying, most the time." I replied.

"Oh, yeah. You're the big runner on campus. I read an article about some race you ran in California last summer."

I laughed. "Yup. That's me... How's school going?"

"I'm graduating at the end of the term. It's been a grind, but I can finally see the end."

"Nice. I've still got a year to go after this."

"It's been a tough road and I'm looking forward to moving on."

"Yeah, me too. Hard to believe that we are this far in though. Seems like yesterday we just got going."

"You got that right." He reached out and we slapped hands. "I should be getting back to my friends. Nice to see you."

"Yeah, see yuh around... Good luck with graduation."

I sat back down and finished my sandwich. I took a deep breath and looked around. I finally felt like I had enough energy to make it back home, but I was also looking forward to cuddling back up on my couch and disappearing from the world for another eight hours.

* * *

I woke to a dark room. Only the green light of the clock across the room on the stove threw a fuzzy light into the atmosphere. I squinted and looked toward the singular light and made out a few blurry numbers, two AM. I stared into the darkness and was amazed by how hungry I was. It was as if my body had devoured every nutrient I had provided it and continued to gnaw away at the inner lining of my stomach. I read an article for one of my Biology classes my freshman year on autocannibalism about a guy who died from his body devouring itself from the inside. I felt like if I didn't feed my body, it too would start devouring itself. So, I gave it what it wanted and, over the next couple of days, I felt my equilibrium returning and my energy level ratchet up.

It was on the fifth morning after the marathon that I woke up with vigor. I felt something had changed inside me. I had an urge to get up and out of my apartment. I didn't have a class until late afternoon, so I called JoJo to see if he wanted to meet at the docks for a run and swim. Fortunately, he didn't have a class on Wednesdays, so we decided to meet at ten.

I arrived at the docks early, eager to get going, something I hadn't felt for months, and really not with this much energy since August. While I waited, I walked out to the end of one of the docks. I stood and watched a few boats go by while the sun warmed the top of my head. I closed my eyes and took a deep breath. I could feel a smile spreading wide across my face and an interesting feeling of both calm and eagerness settling deep within my gut.

JoJo showed up a few minutes later and met me at the end of the dock. "What yuh up to?" He called out, as he walked toward me.

I turned with a start, as his voice jarred me back into reality. "Hey, JoJo. Just enjoying the sun."

"So, why you so eager to run today?

"Just felt like it."

"How far we goin'?"

"Oh, maybe three or four miles. Thought we would hit the trail that leads around the side of the lake."

"Sounds good."

We started off slowly and, after about half a mile, found our stride and hit a comfortable pace.

"Hey, where you goin'," JoJo said with a bit of surprise.

I looked back, and he was a few steps behind. "Whaddya mean?" I replied over my shoulder.

"I thought we were out for an easy jog."

"Sorry. I didn't realize how fast I was going. I've just got a lot of energy today for some reason."

"Well, you might warn a guy first. I might have prepared myself for a battle." He chuckled through labored breathing as he worked to catch up.

"Okay, here's your warning. You up to going to the park and back?

"What's that... about six miles?" He said with a twinge in his voice.

"Something like that. You think you can keep up with me today?

"Now that's the Running Man I've been looking for. You bet your ass I can keep up."

We ran at a decent clip to the park, but picked up the pace and ran harder the second half. And if you asked me, JoJo was struggling to keep up, which made me feel good. I was feeling the marathon flow again—my stride was smooth and my feet bounced buoyantly off the ground as if I was gliding, almost flying just above the dirt trail.

After we returned to the docks we ripped off our shirts and runners and dove into the cool water. We finished our swim and lay on the end of the dock letting the sun dry our bodies. Finally, JoJo asked, "Where'd this come from today?"

"Where did what come from?"

"I mean, this was more like the old you. In fact, I would say even better than the old you."

"I think I'm just ready. I needed some time to heal and I've done that and now there's nothing holding me back."

"Good. I've missed you."

* * *

Over the next month, my strength increased even more, not just recovering from the marathon, but back to what it was at the end of last summer. And, along with my physical strength, I was feeling good psychologically. I was running five days a week and hitting the weight room four days, and was set to run a road race at the beginning of June, my first competition since Nationals.

But, I felt I had one more thing to do before I was fully recovered and ready to compete again.

On the last Friday of May, after my last class of the week, I made my way to the door of a house I had visited just six weeks earlier. I knocked, but this time I knew who was on the other side. A few moments later, Old Man #2 appeared.

"Hello," he said with a nod and a smile. "To what do I owe the pleasure."

"Well, I wanted to see if you had some time to talk."

"Sure. I don't have anything pressing." He stepped back and waved me in. I followed him through a large living room with a stone fireplace and wood from floor to ceiling and then we walked through the kitchen, and then a large, sliding glass door, and onto a large cedar deck that overlooked an expansive yard of green grass and fruit trees.

"Take a seat. I'll grab us a couple waters."

"Thanks, that sounds good."

He returned with two tall glasses, the tinkling of ice could be heard as he set them down on the round glass table that sat in the middle of the deck.

"So, what brings you out my way?"

I took a sip of water and cleared my throat. "I've been thinking a lot over the last few weeks... about the work I've put in and about the goals I have had for myself since I first qualified for Nationals as a freshman. I lost myself after I got injured and never recovered. In fact, I thought about how I could have easily lost my chance to do what I am capable of." I paused for a few seconds. Old Man #2 sat quietly, looking at me, head tilted to the side. "If you and Coach hadn't taken me to the marathon, I don't know if I would have pulled myself out of my rut before it was too late." I paused again. Old Man #2, still quiet, smiled and nodded. "I'm not sure what this means, but you were there when I first broke through. You were the last guy I passed in that race my freshman year and you were there to carry me during the marathon when I was about to fall. And then you urged me to run when I didn't think I could. And... and that last mile or so..." I stopped. I tried to find my words. "That last mile—I—I'm still not sure what happened. I felt almost like I was loose from my own body, like I was weightless, like I was floating. And—and it was your hands and your voice that made it possible."

We sat there. Old Man #2 leaned forward and put his hand on mine. "Nobody ever reaches greatness on their own. There's always other people who help along the way.'

"I know, but you didn't have to do what you did."

"I appreciate it, but I did have to do something. After that first race we ran together I knew you had something special, and as a lover of running, I feel it is important to support young talent. That's actually one of the tenets of our running club, to support and encourage young runners. But even if it wasn't, you deserve the support. And actually, we have one thing in common that made it feel necessary."

"You mean the injury?"

He smiled. "Right. The injury. And I don't want us to have two things in common. I want you to have the chance to use your talent. I didn't have that opportunity, partially because of the injury, but also because of my own short-sightedness. I couldn't let myself walk away without doing what I could to help you get your shot."

"I really appreciate it."

"I know you do. And all I want in return is for you to run."

"Well, I'm doing a lot of that."

"And the other thing, enjoy it. That's why you were able to do so well with the marathon. There were no expectations. No stopwatch. You just ran."

"I get it. That felt really good."

"I know you won't have that situation when you are competing. The time will be ticking away, but look for things to enjoy even during the stressful times. No matter how the race ends, be proud of your preparation. Be proud of your determination. Be proud that you are willing to put yourself on the line and challenge yourself."

"Well, it sure felt good to just run and not worry about anything except finishing the race."

"Yes, it does, and you do it well."

We talked for about an hour and then I looked down and I checked my watch. "I've got to be going, I'm supposed to meet some guys from the team tonight."

"I don't want to keep you from your plans. Thanks for stopping by."

"Before I go, though, I wanted to ask if I could come again sometime."

"Of course. Anytime."

"Thanks. It feels good to talk about running away from the stresses of competition."

"I'm sure it does and I love to talk running, so I'll be looking forward to the next time.

* * *

Throughout my senior year, I visited Old Man #2 a half dozen times. Our conversations were always a great release from the stresses of training and competition and, to tell you the truth, I'm sure his words of wisdom played into my ability to both finish my senior season and graduate seven months later.

Chapter Twenty

Spring ended, my junior year was in the rear view mirror, and three road races carried me through the summer months and into my final preseason. While I didn't have that breakthrough competition like I did the previous summer, the training and competitions that followed the marathon gave me everything I needed going into my final season. Physically, I was exactly where I was a year ago, but mentally I was a step or two ahead. Something about that last mile of the marathon and the conversations with Old Man #2 helped me gain a new understanding of myself and a new appreciation for running.

Day one of preseason and the reality run were just minutes away. I walked with JoJo and the New Guy down the stairs from the locker room and into the corridor that led past the weight room, outside, and onto the track. Twelve months ago I was watching my team run off into the distance while I stayed behind. Now, I would be leading them into battle with a newfound confidence, with a newfound level of understanding. It was not just about competition. It was not just about running to win anymore. It was about running to run—about feeling the ground under my feet—about finding the joy in the endeavor.

We walked down the hallway and through two large, heavy, metal doors. They creaked as we pushed them open and a dim light, just bright enough to show us the way, peeked out from behind the gray clouds above. A rare August drizzle was falling softly, but it was as if I was a wildflower drinking the mist as it hit my petals. I lapped it up and nourished my body. My roots grew stronger, my stem longer.

We met on the track. All seven varsity members returned for a run at a second league title in four years. We had new team members including four freshmen. I looked them up and down as Coach addressed the team. *Did they have what it takes?* I asked silently, turning this old question outwardly, no longer associating it with myself. Coach ended his day-one speech and turned to me, "Okay, they're all yours."

I stepped in front of the group, turned, and paused for a moment. "Well, I have a couple quick things to say before we take off." I paused and looked at them with confidence. "The reality run is not a race. Time doesn't matter. It is a day to enjoy. Use it to find your stride. Find your pace knowing this is the beginning of something good." I looked up and down the line of runners. "Freshmen, I was once in your spot. I was once struggling to keep up, but then, after time, I found my stride. Let today be the start of that journey for you." I smiled, turned, and began to run.

The team fell in behind me.

* * *

Soon, preseason was in the rearview mirror and we were deep into training and our first competition was just around the corner. It was wet, muddy, seven AM. We were rounding the bend, just starting the incline that led to Cardiac Hill. As I turned to my left and started my climb I realized this was going to be more difficult than usual. I looked up and all I could see were streams of water and mud flowing down the middle of the incline. I was planning on pushing hard up the hill and to the finish and then turn to cheer my teammates in. But, after I was halfway up, I stopped, struggling to keep my feet under me. I gained my footing and turned to look behind me. No one was in sight. A few moments later I saw a figure churning up the hill and right behind him, a couple more runners trudging their way up. I started calling their names and urging them forward. I gave them high fives as they passed me and told them I would meet them at the finish. I counted the runners as they passed, four-five... six. A few minutes later seven... and then eight, nine, and ten.

And finally, as numbers eleven and twelve came slowly up the hill, one of them said to me, "A couple guys are struggling back there. I don't think they'll make it. I'm not sure who it is."

"Okay, thanks. I'll check it out. Keep pushing yourself." I ran down to the bottom of the hill about twenty-five meters away. Nobody in sight. I jogged a little farther and found two freshmen struggling to continue. One of them looked to be okay, but was having difficulty keeping the other runner on his feet. "Hey, guys. I'm here to help." I put my hand on the shoulder of the helper. "Why don't you jog on ahead. I've got it here."

"Thanks, Captain," he replied and slowly started the trudge uphill."

I turned to the other runner. "You'll be okay. Let's do this together."

"I don't think I can." A quiet voice struggled through sobs.

"Don't worry," I whispered. "Just put one foot in front of the other. One foot... the next foot... move forward." He began moving, lifting his left foot, then his right. I repeated my whisper, "One foot... the next foot... move forward." We repeated this transaction, over and over again—my whisper... his moving feet.

The hill got steeper. He slipped. I caught him under his armpits and steadied him. "One foot... the next foot... move forward," I whispered again. He struggled to maintain his balance, but we made it to the top together... whisper... moving feet... whisper... moving feet. He stopped, but I grabbed his hand and urged him along. My hand on his—pulling him forward, moving him forward, urging his feet, one and then the other.

We reached the front side of the fieldhouse. I kept his hand, helping him keep his momentum. We rounded the side of the building and the track came into view. He began running on his own and picked up the pace. I let go and ran alongside him as he galloped and then glided the twenty-five meters to the stairs that led down and onto the track. He ran harder as his teammates cheered his efforts. I continued beside him, in stride, as we joined the team together.

* * *

Our first competition came and went. Our team was strong. We swept the meet, beating the other two teams handily, with myself, JoJo, and the New Guy finishing one-two-three. The final meet score was 20 to 40 to 63. It was rare for us to be this strong top to bottom, as we had five upperclassmen and two sophomores on our varsity. Since it was a small meet we were allowed to enter up to ten runners each, and our non-scorers showed well, placing ahead of a number of the other teams, varsity runners.

The next two meets went about the same. They were both small meets, with three teams each. I felt strong, setting a course record in two out of the three meets.

Our first big competition came in the middle of October, an inter-conference meet with ten teams. I was excited because three of the top ten national placers from last year were going to be there. I had been following their times and knew if I ran well, I would have a chance to win. I tried to curb my desire to focus on winning, though, and instead use what I learned in California, from Coach Johnson, and from Old Man #2, finding the joy. I have noticed that focusing more on myself and the act of running, looking for the feeling of floating like I experienced at the end of the marathon helped me reach new heights. So far, I haven't been able to use what I learned from Coach Johnson this year, as I was always in the lead in our first three meets. But, I figured this competition would be different and I was excited to see where I stood at this point in the season.

On the day of the meet the sun struggled to find its way past gray clouds and the ground was soaked from a thunderstorm the previous night. It would be a mud run, a trudge through soggy trails and fields, a real test of toughness and endurance. It would be difficult to find a smooth stride at any point in the race. There was a wide-open start across a compacted grassy field that filtered onto a trail covered in wood chips which made up almost two miles of the race. This would be the battleground. Seasoned runners understand how to jockey for position through tight quarters and I anticipated there would be a lot of that going on. So, I prepared myself for a battle and I was ready to embrace every moment.

As seventy runners gathered at the start, two lines formed, one in front of the other, expanding across the width of the field, with the lead runners on each team finding a spot in the front.

The race began with a solid push through the first half mile, and then the jockeying began as the width of the line squeezed together and we funneled into the narrowing path through the woods.

I found myself shoulder to shoulder with another runner and three others neck-n-neck ahead of us a few paces. I could hear footsteps close behind and knew I had to keep pace. Surprisingly, the pace felt slow and I was waiting for someone to break from the pack, but halfway through the race, the top runners, maybe eight of us, were in a tight group, three in front, me and my shoulder partner, and two or three close behind.

I was running freely, feeling good, but at the same time trying to figure out a strategy. I thought I would be running hard at this point, doing what I had before, using my gaze to pull myself in and pass runners ahead of me, but this was different. It felt like everyone was waiting and I had to figure out if I should go or maintain pace with the group. There wouldn't be much room to pass the runners in front of me until we left the woods and the race opened back up, but that only left me about three-quarters of a mile to make my move.

As I ran, I reminded myself to relax and enjoy the movement of the race. I smiled to myself and felt my feet moving and bounding off the soggy ground. And then, I let my feet do what they wanted to do. I let my legs guide my body and move my feet. I let them do what they have trained to do and what they enjoyed doing.

And, on their own, they quickened the pace. Legs churned faster, feet bounding softly. I was now a few strides ahead of my shoulder partner and on the heels of the three leaders. The runner on the right began to move as he heard my feet closing in. That opened up room for me to slip in line with the other two runners, and then slip passed and hold pace with the runner who had moved ahead.

My legs kept churning and with relative ease, I passed the leader as we exited the woods and hit the open ground. I settled my breathing and focused on the run. I felt my feet bounce, bound, and then glide across the soggy field. My arms swished along my body, one and then the other, in sync with my legs that continued to motor along, faster and faster, without effort.

The finish was in sight. I heard nothing. I felt nothing. I was unmoored from my body.

My feet flew, my arms swished, my mouth smiled as my breath entered and exited steadily.

I crossed the finish and slowly came to a stop. Breathing was slow and in control. My body was relaxed.

Runner number two finished almost a minute behind me, followed by runners three and four, and then a few more, and then one by one the rest of the runners filed in.

Coach approached me as I walked off to the side. He smiled and extended his hand. I met his hand and shook.

"Nice," he said." I smiled back. "Well done." He added.

"Thanks, Coach."

JoJo finished five places behind me followed by the New Guy just a couple spots back. Our fourth and fifth runners finished high enough to help us place second among the ten teams. It was a great test for all of us. Now we had a good idea where we stood as a team and I had proved to myself that finding the joy is what would continue to propel me forward.

* * *

We reached our final hard practice of the season before tapering for the final league meet and national qualifier. We had established a strong varsity team, but there were a couple young runners on our second squad who were knocking on the door and could replace our sixth and seventh runners. Interestingly, one of them was the freshman I helped finish the muddy run up Cardiac Hill early in the season.

We gathered on the track, milling around and waiting for Coach when Trevor, the muddy run freshman, stood next to me quietly. I turned and looked at him. He stood silently.

"Hey." I finally said. "How's it going?"

"Not bad."

"Glad you made it through the season. Looks like you've improved quite a bit."

"Yeah. Thanks. That's what I wanted to talk to you about."

"Oh. What's up?"

"Well," He turned toward me. His eyes glued to the ground. "Well, I want to thank you for helping early on. I don't think I'd still be here if you didn't help me up the hill."

"For sure. I'm glad you're still here. You're looking pretty good."

He smiled and looked away. "I'm not sure what it was, but something happened at the end of that run when you were pulling me along. It almost felt like your energy transferred into me. I couldn't believe how good I felt coming down those stairs." We stood for a moment. "That's what I work on remembering when I run—how I felt coming down those stairs. When you let go of my hand I felt a surge of energy, like I was almost floating."

"I know the feeling. It's amazing, isn't it?"

A whistle blew and pulled our attention to Coach who was standing at the side of the hill that led up to the sidewalk that wrapped around the fieldhouse. We jogged over and listened to another rousing speech and workout instructions—a two-mile partner run through the woods, ending with buddy carries up the fieldhouse hill. "Set your watches. I'll meet you back here in forty minutes," he barked.

"Hey, freshman." I caught myself, "I mean, Kevin. Why don't you partner with me today." I started to jog away. He sped over, met my stride, and we took off, up the stairs, around the fieldhouse, and into the woods.

* * *

Our final meet was with six teams. Our team goal was to take the top three spots, place our final two scorers in the top ten, and our sixth and seventh runners in the top twenty. They allowed three extra runners per team, so a couple of our younger guys were gunning for varsity spots and Kevin was chosen as our tenth runner. He had been improving all season and was performing well in practice the last few weeks, actually finishing in front of a couple of the varsity guys on occasion on some of our longer runs.

Before the race, Kevin told me he was shooting to take the final spot on varsity. He wanted to run at Regionals. As we walked to the starting line, I looked at him and winked. "Remember how it feels to float through the finish." He smiled back.

At the end of the race I had taken first by my largest margin of the season, followed by JoJo and the New Guy. We didn't quite make our team goal—scorer number four came in seventh and scorer number five was eleventh. But, our fifth scorer was Kevin. He ran the race of his life and he now had two weeks before the Regionals to up his game.

It was a difficult decision for Coach, but he moved Kevin onto varsity and gave the tough news to one of our teammates that for some reason was struggling the last few weeks. A few years ago Coach would have kept the upperclassmen on varsity since a team qualifying spot was not in the cards, but now, it was not only in the cards, we had a shot at winning and we even had a shot at a top ten finish at Nationals if everyone was firing on all cylinders.

Chapter Twenty-One

We did what we needed to do at Regionals. I cruised to the finish, two minutes ahead of JoJo, who took second. The New Guy took fourth and our final two scores were in the top twenty. It was now our final practice week of the season. We had three days of recovery workouts and then took off for Nationals on Thursday morning before the Saturday race.

On Friday we visited the course. It was a gloomy day outside, but to me, it felt like the sun was burning bright. We walked around as a team checking every bump and turn. It was the smoothest course I had ever run in college. A wide-open start that slowly narrowed to a trail that was at least five runners wide. There would not be as much jostling for position throughout the race. It would be a true test of pure running.

We took a slow jog through the final two and a half miles. We talked about how to approach different parts of the race—the open start, the wide trail in the middle that undulated up and down slightly, and then opened up to a flat, hardpack field a half mile from the finish.

I broke from the team for half an hour. I spent some time at the starting line, visualizing myself bursting at the sound of the gun and quickly setting a strong pace. I walked to the middle part of the course, the trail that was a little over two miles. I stopped and looked down the trail as far as my eyes could see. I saw myself leading the pack, taking every bump and turn in stride, flying with ease, through the shadows of the trees, the sound of footsteps, behind in the distance.

I took a shortcut to the finish—then jogged through the finish line. I heard the cheers of the crowd. I heard the sound of the announcer's voice booming. I felt my legs moving, the ground underfoot, my deep, easy breaths carrying me to the end. I knew my goal. It was emblazoned in my mind, but I would not say it. Instead, I focused on finding myself in the race—doing what I could to maximize my abilities while enjoying every step, every leg forward, each churning of my arms. I knew this race was built for me—no fighting for position—no jostling through crowds. I could let myself free and do what my mind and body had trained to do since I met Jade almost eight years ago, at the beach, by my house on the lake.

Ever since I met Jade, I have been running. First, to catch up with her as we ran together all over our little town. Then, to find myself as we trained on the trails near my house on the lake and on the trails near the high school with the team and then races against other high schoolers in our league, in our region, and in our state. Next up was Cardiac Hill, running for the first time on my own—away from my house on the lake and everything I knew, without Jade, without my best friend Tim, or my high school teammates, my family hundreds of miles away—finishing that dreaded run with cheers from my new teammates, the ones I would soon find out would now be pushing me to become stronger. Later, I found myself running past Old Man #2, who would become an instrumental part of my development during my final two years of college. I found this out later, as my assistant coach and Old Man #2 abducted me and took me on a self-fulfilling prophecy twenty-six-plus miles in the making. Old Man #2's appearance in my life, I have to believe, was fate. The race with Jade the summer after our sophomore year of college solidified my relationship with the girl I had loved since the summer before high school. Coach Johnson and the California race taught me more in a three-day span than I would have ever thought possible and that trip wouldn't have been a reality without Coach Jay. He paid my way and helped me make connections. Throw in the injuries that plagued me my junior year and the diligent work Ron, our head of physio, did with me through my recovery, and my journey is complete. Each step along the way is important, and the entire time, I was running.

And now I knew. I could feel it. No matter what happened tomorrow at ten AM, I was where I needed to be. I was among my people. I was among others who loved to run. I was among the best in the nation and was given one more chance to step up to the line and prove myself to myself. To prove to myself just how much running means to me. I look back on all that happened to me and feel nothing but gratitude. I feel gratitude for each person who played a role in my development. For each race. For each opponent. For each obstacle.

I stood at that moment, a few feet back from where I would end my college career the next day, and played the image over and over in my head—crossing the line, feeling the joy.

* * *

The next day I woke at six AM. A nervous energy pulsed through my body. JoJo lay in the bed next to me in the hotel room. A dim light made its way from a crack in the curtain across the floor and onto the wall on the far side of the room. I didn't get up. I just listened to the silence. I allowed myself to feel the moment. This is where today begins and I wanted to be in the moment from beginning to end.

I took a few deep breaths, calming the blood that had already started coursing through my body with eagerness. I knew I had to relax and allow time to pass, allow the start time to come at its own pace. My anxiousness would do nothing, but tire me out.

I finally got up and walked to the bathroom and switched on the light. I felt the coolness of the ceramic bowl as I lifted the lid of the toilet, stood, and relieved myself. I flushed, closed the lid, and then turned to the shower and listened to the faint squeak of the single knob in the middle of the wall as I turned it to the left. A hollow splashing quietly filled the small hotel bathroom, reverberating against the walls of the shower stall. I pulled the knob on the faucet and the water worked its way up the pipes and finally out of the nozzle about six feet off the floor. The water made a pattering noise as the spray fell to the ground and streamed toward the drain.

I pulled my underwear off and kicked it in the corner with the toes of my right foot. I turned and stuck my hand under the running water to check the temperature, adjusted the knob slightly, then stepped in and closed the sliding glass door behind me.

I moved forward into the waterfall splashing into the bottom of the tub and let the water run from the top of my head, down my back, buttocks, and legs, and watched as it flowed off my feet and toes and into the drain. I leaned forward, placing my hands on the wall under the shower nozzle, and relaxed my body as my muscles warmed.

I took a deep breath and stood up. I turned and grabbed the shampoo, squeezed a bit onto my hand, and then rubbed it thoroughly into my hair. I found the bar of soap sitting in a small dish on the side wall and rubbed it on my face and body. I then let the water slowly take the suds from my body and into the drain. I watched the little white bubbles swirl, pause, and then get sucked down.

I stood for a moment longer and then reached and turned off the water. I opened the sliding door and took the towel off the hook on the wall. I dried myself off, walked over and used a hand towel to remove the steam from the mirror above the sink. I looked at myself closely and wondered how different I would feel in about four hours, my final college race behind me. I pursed my lips, squinted, and then smiled at myself.

I wrapped the towel around my naked body and walked out into the room. JoJo was sitting at the small round table in the corner next to the window eating a protein bar, an open bottle of water next to him. He had pulled the curtains open and a dim light shone into and across the room.

"You're up," I said in a cheerful voice and smiled.

"You're feeling awfully good this morning," he replied as he stood up and gave me a playful nudge on the shoulder.

"A warm shower can do wonders," I said. He picked up his shaving kit from the dresser next to the TV and made his way into the bathroom. A few minutes later, I heard a squeak of the knob and the water running in the tub.

I used an electric tea kettle to make my pre-competition oatmeal and took a small orange juice from the mini-fridge. With my belly warm and content, I sat on my bed, leaned against the wall and read a book I had brought with me, *Silver Bullet*, by Stephen King. I always carried with me something to read, to both pass the time and help keep my mind calm.

JoJo finished up in the bathroom, came out, and sat on the end of the bed. His hair was still wet and uncombed. "You're not dressed yet?" He questioned.

"No. Just enjoying the morning." I stood up, still in my towel. Set my book on the bed and stretched my hands up in the air. I let out a refreshing yawn, walked over to my bag by the dresser, and laid my uniform and sweats on the bed.

Over the next twenty minutes, we chatted and dressed. We talked about how the season had gone and how we were looking forward to the race. It was overcast, but not raining. In fact not much rain had fallen in the last few days, so the course would be relatively dry. We knew it was an ideal day to test ourselves.

At seven twenty-five we headed down to meet the team. Coach was standing outside the van at the front entrance of the lobby. The exhaust was faint, but made a steady stream out of the tailpipe that rose and disappeared into the distance as the engine idled. Coach greeted us as everyone began to arrive and load.

By the time we got to the race site, it was less than two hours until we were called to the starting line. Coach always liked us to be early, so we could acclimate to the environment. We spent a while getting to know the course the day before, but he always wanted us to be comfortable the day of.

We spent a long while walking the grounds around the course, feeling the cool air and the mist that hovered just above our heads. We went for a jog from the start into the first part of the trails leading into the woods and then cut to the end of the course and jogged to the finish. Finally, we spent a few minutes doing individual preparations.

I spent time visualizing myself taking the lead from the start and bursting into the woods, increasing my pace with each stride. I felt good. I felt prepared. I could feel my feet bounding, my legs churning, my arms propelling me forward. I saw myself breaking through the tape at the finish and then turning to see the line of runners finishing after.

I looked down at my watch, fifteen minutes until first call. I walked over to an orange Gatorade jug, filled a small paper cup with water, and drank. I could feel the cold liquid slide down my throat. I repeated this one more time and turned to jog back to the team. Just then, I heard my name called.

I looked over my shoulder and a familiar face, one I hadn't seen in over a year, jogging toward me.

"Geno," I called to him once I had turned his direction. My friend from the California run trotted up to me. We clasped hands and pulled in for a bro hug.

"You're looking good, my man," Geno beamed.

"Great to see yuh, man."

"Yeah, you too, but I'm really just scoping out the competition," he laughed.

"Well, your competition's feeling good." I met his laugh.

"Wish we had more time to catch up." He reached out and we slapped hands.

"Yeah, I'm planning on heading back out to California after graduation," I assured him.

"Looking forward to it."

"Have a great race." We began to jog our separate ways. I turned back and jogged in place, "Geno," I called to him. He turned around. "Meet me at the finish line." I gave him a thumbs up.

"You got it." He smiled, turned, and trotted the other way. I stood and watched him jog off, remembering the good times we had that warm August weekend with Coach Johnson and his track club.

I began my slow jog back to my team. My thoughts narrowed.

I looked at my watch—eleven minutes until first call. I took three deep breaths and centered my focus. I felt my body as I jogged. My muscles were relaxed and warm. There was nothing more to do, but wait.

I circled up with my team. Everyone was standing and stretching or jumping up and down and loosening their muscles. I stood, legs wide apart, hands on my hips, and circled my hips one way and then the other. I circled my arms to loosen my shoulders. I took a deep breath.

Coach pulled us in close and gave us a few last words. I would like to say I heard what he was saying, but I was in my own world. My vision was narrowed. I only heard my own voice in my head—*Explode, Relax, Enjoy.* This was my goal for the day. When the gun sounded, I would shoot off the starting line and explode into the race, staying relaxed and enjoying each and every step. I would be connected to every stride, with every movement, with every breath, until I was no longer connected. I would be out of body, flying through the course.

Finally, the first call came and we headed toward the starting line. We met another 250 runners at the wide-open start. We were in starting block thirteen, a little right of center.

I had scoped out the start and knew exactly how to attack the race. As the course turned to the left and headed to the trails, I should be in the perfect spot to funnel with a few others into the meat of the course and then let myself go.

I stood, JoJo to my right, the New Guy to my left, the other four members of our team right behind. "On your mark," a voice boomed over the loudspeaker. I crouched slightly. BANG... the gun went off and I shot out, swift and strong. My legs churned, my feet bounced off the compacted grass. I lifted my knees, I swung my arms. I allowed my stride to take form.

I was shoulder to shoulder with a mass of runners, then quickly moved ahead—one stride, two strides, and then a few more. I was in complete connection with myself, focused as I bounded in front, then followed the slight left turn, and slipped onto the trail that led through the woods.

I felt my feet moving faster. I felt the wind blowing by. I heard a voice whisper in my ear, "Move forward. One foot. The next foot. Move forward." I ran. I bound. I flew. My feet were off the ground. I felt nothing. I heard nothing. I was both connected, but also a spectator, watching myself glide through the course effortlessly.

The course wound one way and then the next, up slightly and then down. I emerged from the trail and onto the open field, the finish line in sight. I continued to move forward—I continued to fly. I felt a smile spread across my face. I heard the muffled cries of spectators.

I spent the last eight years working to get where I was at that exact moment in time. It had all come together. I was where I wanted to be, doing what I wanted to do, and I enjoyed every stride, every breath.

* * *

After the race, I found Geno among the throngs of people. We slapped hands, smiled, and hugged. We congratulated each other and had a quick conversation about meeting up in the summer when I made it out to California.

I made my way to my team and we ran around the course slowly, talking, laughing, and cooling our bodies. JoJo and the New Guy jogged next to me. Kevin, the freshman, with new experiences, with, I'm sure, new goals to chase, running as part of our pack. We were still a team and always would be. We had a connection—a connection that few will understand— the connection only brought on by miles and miles of strain, stress, and fatigue shared together. A bond that, many years later, would draw us together a few more times, to run, to share stories. And yes, it is running that will draw us together again.

But soon, I will go my own way and watch them finish out their college careers from afar.

Chapter Twenty-Two

Nine months later, I stood on a bluff overlooking the waters of the Pacific. The sun shone bright in the blue skies and waves crashed in the distance. Small boats made their way across the horizon. Gulls swooped to and fro, squawking as they swept to the ground and back into the air.

I heard my name called. I turned to see Jade, followed by Geno and two other runners wearing matching navy blue tank tops, WC Elite Track in bold letters across their chests, covered by numbered bibs. They were making their way toward me. "You ready?" she called. "The race is about to begin."

I peered back at the water and then jogged over to the group. "Yup," I replied. "Just enjoying the scenery." She took my hand and we walked with our new teammates to the starting line.

Also by Adam C. France

The World Hovering Around Me

The story follows a teenager who becomes homeless after he is disowned by his parents when he reveals he is gay. Readers are taken on a heart-wrenching journey as he battles for his life, finds love, and eventually becomes a force for change in his community.

Fighting For Loose Change

The story explores the emotional entanglement and self-discovery of a character with an addictive personality searching for a way to fulfill the impulses that govern his life. Follow him as he graduates from the field behind the apartments, to a state title, to the dark underbelly of the fight world. Experience the visceral struggles as he battles his opponents, as well as the desires that course through his body and mind.